SCOUSE G
2

BLOOD BROTHERS... AND SISTERS

IAN MCKINNEY

YOUCAXTON PUBLICATIONS

OXFORD & SHREWSBURY

SCOUSE GOTHIC
2

Blood Brothers... and Sisters

CONTENTS

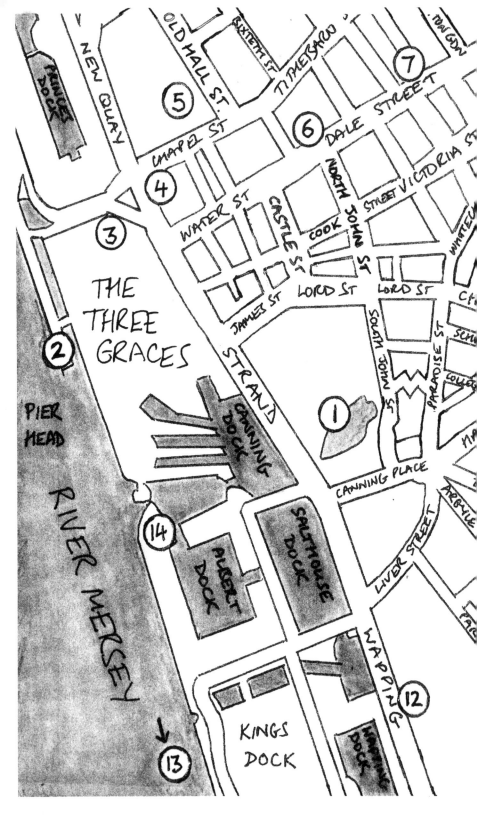

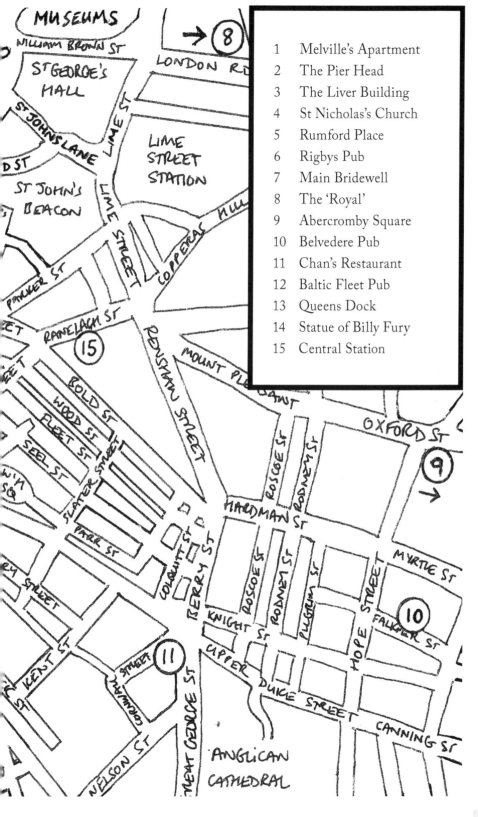

1 Melville's Apartment
2 The Pier Head
3 The Liver Building
4 St Nicholas's Church
5 Rumford Place
6 Rigbys Pub
7 Main Bridewell
8 The 'Royal'
9 Abercromby Square
10 Belvedere Pub
11 Chan's Restaurant
12 Baltic Fleet Pub
13 Queens Dock
14 Statue of Billy Fury
15 Central Station

– 1 –

The Royal

BEEP!

Sheryl didn't know what it was but she always heard that noise in her dreams. Somehow it seemed louder today.

Usually everything was black and silent—until the dreams returned. Dark, strange dreams, faces from the past and present taunted her, memories and fantasies combined in a nightmarish kaleidoscope.

BEEP!

One minute she was laying on the pavement overwhelmed by pain, the taste of blood in her mouth, the sounds of screams and sirens in her ears.

Then someone was shining a light in her eyes and she was unable to talk or move a muscle.

BEEP!

Another image: helpless handcuffed to a chair… a man with a knife. She shuddered at the memory. That dream always frightened her the most. Although today it was different—she felt the shudder through her bones. Every other time the shudder had only happened in her head.

BEEP!

The nightmare faded, replaced by Lee's face smiling. Where was he? Was he safe? She needed to warn him. She

I

tried to call to him but she had no voice. She shouted inside but nothing happened, tried to move — but her limbs were heavy.

BEEP!

She made out faint voices and tried to call again, but still they couldn't hear her.

'Thanks for giving me a hand with the beds, Tash. It's been a shit shift. Two off with flu and one from the agency who doesn't know her arse from her elbow. Don't know why I bother. I'm goin' home to watch '*Corrie*' with a large glass of wine. Hope you have a quiet night luv.'

BEEP!

'This one won't cause you no trouble. Quiet as a mouse she is — poor thing.'

'What happened to her?'

'Fell five stories — no one knows if she jumped or was pushed — it was that block of flats that had the explosion off London Road.'

BEEP!

'There's no name on her chart, Shaz.'

'Don't know who she is, that's why. No ID, nothin'- just found on the pavement with handcuffs on. Bizzies are waiting until she's conscious to find out who she is and what happened. Can you turn off that drip alarm? It's doin' me 'ead in.'

'That better?'

'Yep, thanks Tash. I've gorra poundin' 'eadache.'

'Are these her drugs on the side? Why haven't they been done yet?'

'Too busy, an' that new house officer hasn't signed them off yet, She was supposed to have those sedatives an hour ago but he's nowhere to be seen.'

'Where is the lazy git?'

'Where do you think? Sniffing around that new Staff nurse on Ward 6 with the big boobs.'

'Pity about this one's hair—the poor thing.'

'Think that was the least of their worries, Tash. She was a right mess when they brought her in—'ead injury, broken limbs and smashed hands. Had to sedate her then give her five units of blood too. Bizzies couldn't even take her finger prints. Look at 'er now, you'd never think it was only a week ago.'

'A week? That scar's nearly healed?'

'It's coz of her excellent care.'

They both laughed.

A door closed; it was silent again.

Sheryl tried to piece together what she had just heard. She was in hospital it seemed and she'd been there a week and they didn't know who she was. Where was Lee? Was he safe? When they came back she'd try to talk to them, get them to warn Lee. But then again—what was that they'd said about an explosion and the police wanting to know who she was? She couldn't let them take her fingerprints—they might still be in their files.

If Lee didn't know where she was, he couldn't rescue her and she couldn't warn him that there was another vampire after him. That left one option: she'd have to escape on her own.

Melville leaned on the bar sipping his Liver Bird cocktail. He finished it and took the green olive from the cocktail stick and lined it up with the other two on the bar counter in front of him. An untouched cocktail with a bright red maraschino cherry stood next to the line of olives.

He waved to the barman, who came over.

'Another?' asked the barman.

Melville nodded, pealed a note from the bundle in his money clip and placed it on the bar next to a pile of change. The barman took the note and returned with another cocktail and more change.

'Stood you up again?'

'Looks like it.' Melville pushed the change towards the barman. 'Have one yourself.'

'Thanks,' the barman picked through the change and selected a few coins.

'Take it all.' Melville was used to using dollar bills and he found the currency confusing—When had they go rid of pounds shillings and pence? He turned on the bar stool and scanned the room, which was almost as busy as the first time they'd met. People laughed and flirted; a hundred separate dramas played out in front of him. He felt like an observer, not part of this city—or this time.

In the past he would have looked on this moment as an opportunity for an easy kill. He watched a group over the far side of the room where a young woman sat on the arm of a large sofa, playing with the stirrer in her cocktail and looking around for an excuse to leave the rowdy group she was with. Melville studied her dispassionately, not as a person but as a fresh 'Emma' to add to his collection.

He sipped his drink and she looked in his direction and caught his eye. He knew what she was looking for but he wasn't interested tonight. He turned away but not before he'd noticed her disappointment, and he thought to himself that she would never appreciate how close she had come to death. For the first time in his life, he too was looking for someone to whisk him away—but where was she?

It was just over a week since her disappearance and for the first day or so he'd expected her to return any minute with an amusing tale to tell, but then, as they days went by, he began to look for her. He wasn't worried for her safety for obvious reasons but he needed to know what had happened to her—and why she'd left him. She hadn't given any indication that she was bored or intended to move on but neither had she explained were she'd been living when they'd first met. Perhaps she'd gone back to someone else?

He'd taken to going out every evening to visit their old haunts, hoping to catch a glimpse of her in the crowds, and he always ended each evening here at this bar. He stirred his cocktail and smiled as he remembered how she'd appeared out of the crowd and asked him for a drink all those weeks ago. Where was she? He really missed her. It was so many years since he'd had a longing for another human being that didn't involve blood. Why had she gone? Was she bored with him? She said he was boring—called him 'Soft lad'. He'd always thought she was joking. Perhaps she'd found someone better and moved on?

That was what came with being a vampire—always having to move on. If you stayed somewhere too long, people asked about your past and wondered why you didn't age. Or the authorities took an interest in all the missing persons. Perhaps that was it: she'd gone looking for more excitement and fresh 'hot dates'.

Deep down he was worried as to how he'd react if he found her with someone else. He'd want to be friendly but cool. He knew that he wouldn't be able to deceive her and he didn't want to make a fool of himself. What would she do if he begged her to return—laugh at him?

He finished the cocktail and lined up the last olive with the other three. He'd always been a fool where women were concerned, always fell head over heels in love, always thought it would last forever, and always imagined that they felt the same way. Perhaps Sheryl was the same as the others? He stabbed the olives with his cocktail stick — *Isabella* — *Beatrice* — *Charlotte* — *Sheryl* — then popped them in his mouth and swallowed them one by one. He picked up the cocktail he'd bought for Sheryl, took out the cherry and drank it down in one then looked at the cocktail stick in his hand with its single maraschino cherry. It shone bright red and glistened under the artificial light of the bar like a small beating heart and he thought — and *Emma.* Suddenly he lost his appetite, dropped the cherry into the empty glass and left the bar.

He walked aimlessly around the Ropewalks where the streets were busy with people moving on to the clubs. He'd planned to visit her favourite club that night but now he changed his mind and walked up the hill out of the centre. He suddenly had the desire to visit '128' and soon he was standing in the street outside. He'd not been there since that night with Sheryl; there had been no need.

Things had changed; the estate agent's board had been replaced by a builder's sign and the front of the house was covered in scaffolding. A battered yellow skip stood in the road outside filled with rubble and rotten timber. Rather than upsetting him, the scaffolding comforted him; the house would have new life with a new family, a fresh start. It would no longer be Charlotte's house.

On impulse he looked into the skip in the street below the scaffolding. It was difficult to make much out under the rubble but then he saw the glint from something shiny. He reached into the skip and pulled out an old, brass door-knocker in the shape of a dolphin. It was well worn and its hinge had broken which that was not doubt why it had been discarded. He stroked the dolphin and remember how it used to gleam on Charlotte's front door. How many times had he knocked on it and waited patiently to see Charlotte's smiling face?

§

It was late December 1917 and over four months since Henry's death, and Melville had just returned to Liverpool on Christmas leave after being presented with his VC by the King. His photograph had been in *The Times* and had been reproduced in the local papers together with that of his dead friend, Noel Chavasse. Any good news from the front was eagerly seized upon among the war-weary population, doubly so if the news related to the King's Regiment. Consequently he had become a local celebrity and had been met at Lime Street Station by a small group of dignitaries eager to have their photographs taken with him. Only after posing with them and agreeing to attend a civic function later that evening had he managed to slip away to Charlotte's house.

Now that Henry was dead there was no need for a divorce and no reason why Melville and Charlotte could not marry. He had written to Charlotte several times along these lines since Henry's death but had received no reply, and so it was with a mixture of excitement and trepidation that he knocked at her door.

He waited for what seemed an eternity. He had planned what he would say carefully and rehearsed it many times on his train journey that morning. 'Tongues would wag' and they would obviously be shunned by many of their friends, but he could offer her a new life in America, he would tell her. He was financially secure and she would want for little. He would resign his commission and they could take the next boat to New York. They would arrange for her solicitors to sell the house and sort out the legal niceties, and anything that she wanted to keep could be shipped later. It was exactly what they had dreamed about during their affair when the prospect of a divorce had seemed so unattainable; he knew this was what she had wanted — they could be happy at last.

The door opened and there was Charlotte. She stood silently, as beautiful as when he'd last seen her but sadder. Her eyes that had flashed brilliantly like emeralds when they were alone were now a dull and muddy green. She stepped aside to let him enter but when he tried to kiss her she turned and offered him only her cheek. He knew immediately that things had changed. They had begun with polite indifference on her part, then they had been friends, then confidants and finally lovers — now it seemed the best he could hope for was to remain friends.

They sat in the front parlour and there played out a very English scene. She asked about his health and his plans for the future, and he answered each question politely. Whenever he tried to discuss more personal matters, she cut him short and changed the subject. He knew what she wanted to know and that she was too afraid to ask it: how did Henry die?

It was as she was pouring the tea that she broke down in tears and then he tried to hold her but she pushed him away. She wiped her eyes on a lace handkerchief and tried to pass the cup and saucer to him but her hand shook too much. He took it from her, placed it back on the table and decided to tell her what had happened. He didn't tell her everything, just an abridged version of the truth: Henry had not suffered, had died a hero's death and he, Melville, wasn't responsible. Once he'd finished they sat in silence for many minutes. Almost a hundred years later, he could still remember how the ticking of the mantelpiece clock had seemed deafening in the icy silence. Then she stood up and offered him her hand, thanked him for taking the time to visit her — and for being such a good friend to them both. She wished him well with his future plans and showed him the door.

Their love had died along with Henry. He immediately returned to his regiment at the front line and the chaos of war. Almost two months later, he was notified of Charlotte's death in a letter from Henry's younger brother, Charles, which had been forwarded several times. It explained that Charlotte had been overcome with grief after the death of her beloved husband and had committed suicide. She'd run a hot bath then cut her wrists with one of Henry's razors. The warm water had stopped the clotting and she'd bled to death. She'd apparently left a suicide note but the spilled bath water had caused the ink to run and it had been illegible. Charles's letter went on to say how surprised everyone had been by her suicide because Charlotte had seemed to be coping well after her husband's tragic death.

Melville began to make plans to return to Liverpool then realised that there was no point. Charlotte was dead and buried and his reappearance would only cause gossip and sully her reputation.

He burned the letter and began a new life.

§

Melville looked at the broken dolphin door-knocker and considered taking it home as a keepsake then threw it back into the skip. It should stay in the past with his memories. He walked slowly back down the hill towards his apartment deep in thought. He now knew that he and Charlotte would never have worked; a vampire couldn't live with a mortal. He should have known back then—he'd tried it before. How do you explain not ageing? And how do you explain the killings? Perhaps that was why he fell for Sheryl; she wasn't like anyone he'd ever loved before. He'd hoped that 'forever' really could come true for them both—but it seemed that was not to be.

He kept a photograph of Charlotte in his 1918 diary but he had nothing to remember Sheryl by, nothing—not even a photo. Perhaps it was time to move on, to start yet another new life somewhere else? Where had Sheryl gone? Did she want a fresh start too? And why leave without saying anything? Why leave all her things behind? Her sudden disappearance still disturbed him.

The day she went missing had been like many others. He'd gone for his walk in the morning and in the afternoon Sheryl had gone shopping while Michelle cleaned the apartment. It was only after Michelle left that he'd realised that his phone was missing. He'd searched the lounge thinking that maybe Michelle had moved it and then he'd realised that it must have fallen out of the window. He'd searched the park below and found a few scraps of plastic but nothing else. He wasn't worried—he hardly used his phone; he didn't even know his phone number. Sheryl had bought it so that she could keep in touch with him. He expected her to return soon and was unconcerned.

After she'd been missing for two days, he bought a new phone and searched the apartment until he found her phone number, but all he got when he phoned it was an answering-machine message. He left several messages over the next few days but no response.

On the third day he searched her things for clues as to her disappearance. He felt uneasy doing this. It was like reading someone's diary and he dreaded what he might find. After a cursory look at her clothes and make-up he found her large, inlaid, jewellery box and a well-thumbed Bible, the book-plate inside stated that it was given to Shirley Bernadette Malone on the occasion of her First Holy Communion, the 6th April 1948. Folded inside the back cover there was a small child's drawing of a cat, called 'Monty' by someone named Jeanie.

The jewellery box was locked, but he had spotted a small key next to the old soaps at the bottom of her underwear drawer. He sat on the edge of the bed and emptied its contents onto the duvet. Most of it appeared to be costume jewellery, large colourful gems and thick gold bands. A small drawer inside the box contained a few wedding and engagement rings, a single gold sovereign and a padlock key with a numbered tag. He took the padlock key and was replacing the jewellery piece by piece when he noticed that a pair of large, green, pendant earrings had a maker's mark on them. He went into the lounge and found his magnifying glass. The maker's mark read *Tiffany & Co* and the earrings were hallmarked. He carefully checked each piece. It was all genuine; there was nothing fake about Sheryl Malone or her jewellery.

The following morning he was at a large, old warehouse opposite Queens Dock where a shiny new sign proclaimed: 'Storage-4-U, competitive rates, weekly or monthly rental'. The entrance was at the rear of the building alongside the loading bay and a car park. Next to the main door there was a small office. Inside, a middle-aged woman was in the middle of a long and fruitless conversation, attempting to sell storage to an indecisive client. She put down the phone and shrugged.

'Hiya luv- can I help you?'

'I really hope so. I'm in trouble with my girlfriend. I came in the other day and I think I've put her new shoes in our locker by mistake.'

'No problem, luv. What's your name?'

'Lee Melville. But it's in her name — Sheryl Malone.' He held out the key. 'It's locker A-473.'

'Shouldn't let you, luv — she needs to sign in. But I wouldn't want to ruin your love life — just sign your name there and put her's next to it.'

Melville signed then he thought of something.

'She asked me to check when the rental ends.'

'A-473?' She taped on the keyboard. 'Ten months left; she paid a year up front.'

Once in the warehouse, Melville followed the signs to A-473. He now knew that she had intended to stay in Liverpool but that hardly helped. The mystery was deeper if anything. Perhaps she had another life and lover in the city? That would explain where she went every day when he thought she was shopping.

A-473 was at the end of an aisle. He unlocked the padlock and opened the yellow steel door. Inside there was a single, cardboard box and a hockey-stick case. Nothing else, hardly enough to warrant renting such a large locker; perhaps she'd come and taken what other things might have been there before she disappeared and this was what she didn't need or want.

The box contained old letters from family and lovers, a few small photo albums and a pile of faded Polaroid photos. In one, Sheryl was wearing white hot-pants and a green top tied at the midriff and she was leaning on red sports car. He took the photo and put it in his pocket; at least now he would have a photo to remember her by. Amongst the papers he found an American wedding certificate and a couple of death certificates. He replaced the documents and checked the hockey-stick case. Inside, wrapped in a silk shawl, was a Japanese Samurai sword together with a small, ornate dagger. The sword was nearly a metre long, the black lacquer scabbard decorated with gold butterflies and the intricately carved handle and guard inlaid with silver. He withdrew the sword slowly and it made a gentle 'Ssssh'. The blade was beautifully polished and razor-sharp. He weighed it in his hand and carefully re-sheathed it. The dagger was only about twenty centimetres long but just as beautiful and deadly, its silver scabbard engraved with a dragon motif and the blade honed to perfection. These were no tourist keepsakes but ancient swords with real history. He carefully replaced them in the hockey-stick case and locked the unit.

That evening in the apartment, he considered his options. He decided to try to find her again because he now had a photo that he could show people. Though faded, it was obviously her — there was no mistaking that smile. He put the Polaroid in his jacket pocket and headed into town.

It was another fruitless night. The closest he got to a lead was when a barman in a new club he hadn't been to before thought he'd seen someone like her a few days before but wasn't entirely sure. The general consensus seemed to be that if the girl in the photo wanted to find him she would and there were plenty more fish in the sea, neither of which opinions was particularly reassuring.

He walked back to the apartment in the early hours. The temperature had dropped since he'd set out in the evening and he began to wish he'd worn a thicker coat. He pulled his jacket tightly around him and turned up the collar. What was it with this country? It was supposed to be spring? He decided to cut through Chavasse Park and use the side entrance to the apartments rather than risk the cold winds blowing off the Mersey at the main entrance.

He was approaching the side entrance when he saw movement in the bushes at the edge of the park. Even though he had excellent night vision, a side effect of his 'curse', he couldn't make out what was moving since it was hiding inside the bush. Probably a fox or even a badger he thought but, as he went to open the door with his key-fob, he thought he heard a voice.

The longer Sheryl lay there, the clearer her head became; the sedatives were wearing off. She needed to make sure that they didn't sedate her again if she was going to escape. She tried again and, with difficulty, was able to open her eyes. The room was brightly lit and she could hear noises coming from the corridor outside. If she didn't act now they'd be back to give her the drugs and who knew when she'd next have a chance at freedom. She tried to move her body; the left arm felt heavy and the muscles didn't seem to want to respond, but the right arm moved easily.

She held her right hand in front of her face. The fingers were bandaged and a tube was taped onto the back of her hand. She followed the tube with her eyes and found that it was connected to a drip hanging behind her bed. To her right there was a low table with a small glass bottle and a syringe in a cardboard tray. Perhaps this was the sedative they hadn't had time to give her. What could she do? If she told them she was awake then they'd call the police, but if she did nothing they'd sedate her again. She needed to dispose of the drugs.

Taking a deep breath she rolled on her right side and discovered the reason for her left arm's reluctance. Hand and arm were held together with a large, metal framework, hinged at the elbow, with metal rods screwed directly into the bones. Painfully and with difficulty she twisted around and sat on the edge of the bed and then she got another unpleasant surprise: there was a plaster cast on her left leg. Opposite there was a small sink with a mirror above it. She stretched to the side so that she could see her reflection and was shocked by what she saw. Her head had been shaved and a large, crescent-shaped scar, held together with metal staples, ran across the left hand side of her scalp.

The voices outside seemed to be getting louder; she needed to act quickly. She picked up the squat, glass bottle with her right hand and transferred it to her left, managing to wedge it between her pinned first finger and thumb, and then, taking the syringe, drew up the liquid in the bottle and squirted it into the sink. The next bit was more difficult; she pulled herself upright on the edge of the bed and lunged towards the sink. Supporting herself with her left arm, she turned on the tap and gradually filled the syringe with water, which she squirted back into the glass bottle, replacing it and the empty syringe in the cardboard tray.

She was back in bed with her eyes closed when the door opened and someone entered.

'Hi luv, back at last. I know you can't hear me but it seems rude not to speak to you. Sorry it's taken so long but I've been waiting for *Dr Do-little* to sign your drugs off. He's been trying to get his leg over on Ward 6, but he's back now with a flea in his ear.'

Sheryl could hear the table being moved.

'Just pop this in your line and you'll be off to the land of nod again.'

Sheryl felt the cold liquid flowing into her veins.

'He won't get anywhere with *Barbie* though, I've heard she prefers girls. I'll tell you because I know you won't tell anyone — but I wouldn't tell him. He thinks the sun shines out of his arse and all the women are gagging for it. It's funny watching him trying to smarm his way into her knickers and getting the cold shoulder. I'll pop in and check on you in an hour or so and we can have another chat. Night, night and sweet dreams.'

She heard the door close and voices in the corridor outside, she needed to act now. She sat on the edge of the bed, pulled the drip out of her wrist and tried to stand. Her legs felt weak and the plaster cast made walking difficult but she hobbled over to the door, opened it slightly and listened, then she leaned out and checked the corridor; it was empty. She needed to take stock of things: she was naked save for a paper gown that tied at the back, had a plaster cast on one leg, scaffolding on one arm and a shaved head. Unless she'd slept for many months and it was now Halloween she'd be conspicuous.

She crept down the corridor, the plaster cast 'clunking' as she walked, and took a lift to the ground floor. The visitors had all left and the hospital was quite quiet but she needed an excuse to be seen moving around. There was a wheelchair beside the lift and, in a laundry trolley, she found a blanket. She wrapped the blanket over her shoulders and wheeled herself in the wheelchair to the front entrance. It was NHS policy that no one could smoke on hospital premises consequently patients who wanted to smoke were obliged to do so outside the hospital grounds. She joined a good-natured throng huddled by the main entrance and scrounged a cigarette. After that, all she had to do was to gradually wheel herself to the edge of the group and then disappear into the darkness.

It was late and the area around the hospital quiet and she made steady progress through the hospital grounds, keeping to the shadows, and was soon in Pembroke Place. Then it was all downhill into Liverpool city centre, but first she needed to check on something she'd overheard. Part way down London Road she turned left into a side street. The block of flats once so familiar, was almost unrecognisable, the outside was covered in scaffolding and tarpaulins, the top floor was missing and the concrete was blackened by fire.

Puzzled, she wracked her brain trying to remember everything that had happened before she jumped, but the memories were vague and confusing. The sound of a siren brought her back to reality and she continued her journey downhill towards the illuminated Liver Birds and home.

An hour later, she was freezing cold and hiding in a large shrub on the edge of Chavasse Park. She'd tried buzzing the apartment but no reply. Lee must be out clubbing when he should have been moping around at home and worrying about her—she'd make sure he didn't get to forget that in a hurry. If she went to the front entrance the concierge would let her in but how to explain her appearance? And no doubt by tomorrow the *Echo* would report her escape or more likely report it as an abduction. She huddled under her blanket behind the bush and silently cursed Lee.

Nearly two hours later and almost blue with the cold, she spotted him walking through the park. She crept through the undergrowth until she was close to the side door, using a tree to shield her from the security lights. Lee reached into his pocket for his key-fob to open the door.

'Psst! Soft lad.'

He paused, then changed his mind and went to open the door.

'Oy!! Over here deaf lugs.'

He turned, walked towards the bushes and peered into the shadows.

'Sheryl? — where've you been?'

Even though he could see perfectly in the dark she was crouching down so low that he couldn't get a clear look at her. He walked towards her shrub with his arms outstretched.

'Come here; I've missed yo ...'

'Stay right where you are! Don't you dare come any closer.'

'Why?'

'I've only got on a paper gown with a gap down the back and no knickers.'

Melville smiled: 'I've seen you without knickers before.'

'Yes Lee, but unless you do what I tell you to do, that memory is all you'll have. Go inside and get me big fur coat, me Russian hat with the ear flaps and me right hand Ugg boot.'

'Only the right one?'

'Just do it!'

Melville returned with the clothes and left them to the right of the shrub then stepped back as instructed. A few moments later she emerged like a small, furry mammal from the undergrowth. He rushed over and hugged her.

'Ow! Watch me *Meccano*!'

'What?'

'Let's get inside, Soft lad, then I'll explain.'

He could hear her singing in the bath. Gathering up her clothes that were in a pile outside the bathroom door, he knocked on the door and asked: 'Want anything else?'

'God luv you, Lee; a cocktail and a tool-kit.'

SCOUSE GOTHIC 2

Melville was confused by the tool-kit it must be some sort of joke. He often didn't understand these things so he ignored it and went to make the cocktail. He returned with a 'Liver Bird' with three maraschino cherries, knocked again and entered. Sheryl was sitting in a bath full of bubbles with her left leg in a plaster cast sticking out of the bubbles and propped on the side and with a totally shaved head.

'What happened to you?'

'Latest fashion, Lee — hair is so last year.' She took the cocktail from him. 'Aaah — three cherries, you really know how to spoil a girl.'

'Why did you want a tool-kit?'

'Thought you could un-bolt me *Meccano*.' She lifted her arm from beneath the bubbles.

'I don't understand? Where've you been? What happened?'

She drank the cocktail in one and handed him the empty glass.

'It's a three-cocktail story, Lee. The faster you make them the faster I'll tell it.'

He took her glass to get another one and she turned her head showing the scar on the opposite side and pointed to the staples.

'Don't forget your wire cutters, hun.'

Three cocktails later they were sitting in bed. He had his arm around her and the *Meccano*, staples and plaster cast had all gone. Her warm body nestled next to his; he felt complete.

'Did he tell you his name?' he asked.

'No, I thought you'd know who it was.'

'Can't think of anyone — they've all been "Emmas".'

'He was definitely *not* an "Emma".' She snuggled closer. 'If you think the explosion killed him, perhaps we'll never know.'

'Hope so — he was a sick bastard.'

'I've missed you.' He squeezed her shoulder and kissed her on her bald head.

'You too, Lee. Know what I feel like when I've had some fresh blood?'

'No — what?' Then he felt a roaming hand under the covers.

She giggled, 'Perhaps it's easier to show you, Soft lad.'

The following morning Melville slipped quietly out of bed, leaving Sheryl snoring. An hour later he was back with a carrier bag and she was still asleep. He made coffee, warmed up some croissants, and took her breakfast in bed. A short while later they were sitting in bed finishing the breakfast and he handed her the carrier bag.

'Home coming present.'

Sheryl looked in the bag smiled and took out a blonde wig.

'I haven't been blonde for yonks,' she giggled and put it on.

'Suits you.'

'Don't look too much like Dolly Parton, do I?'

Melville looked her up and down, smiling: 'I see what you mean.'

'You're supposed to be looking at the wig not me boobs.'

She punched him on the arm and he put his arm around her. She snuggled closer.

'They say blondes have more fun. Want to put that to the test, Soft lad?'

He felt her roaming hand again.

'How much blood did they give you?' he asked.

'Plenty. Umm,—not such a *soft* lad after all.'

By mid-afternoon they were eating in a Lebanese restaurant on Bold Street. Sheryl was on her third plate of food, while Melville drank a mint tea and wondered how she could fit it all in.

'Don't look at me like that, Lee. I haven't eaten for a week and I need some energy.'

'I'm the one who needs the energy—now you're back.'

She winked: 'Let's go to the wig shop; you can spend the night with a saucy red-head.'

He left her trying on wigs at a shop in Bold Street and headed back to the apartment with her shopping bags. He was walking down College Lane when he saw that a new barber's shop had opened next to their favourite 'deli'. It was like something from the past, furnished in a *retro* style with plenty of chrome and neon signs. However the staff were very much from the present—young, tattooed and pierced—and most of the clientele seemed to have beards. In the chair closest to the window a man was having a wet shave with a cut-throat razor. It was many years since he'd last been shaved by a barber and Melville suddenly felt nostalgic—he hadn't shaved that this morning so entered the shop.

He sat in the red leather chair while the barber lathered up a badger-hair brush on a block of soap and brushed it over his chin. The barber tilted the chair back and opening the cut-throat razor, placed his hand on Melville's cheek. Melville closed his eyes and the blade skimmed over his face.

§

It was August 1917, Melville was in the underground dug-out attempting to shave by the light of a small oil lamp. It was late but they had orders to move to the forward positions before daybreak and he had decided to shave first. His platoon had been selected to undertake reconnaissance along the Menin Road which they all knew would be a particularly hazardous assignment. Melville had fought enough wars to recognise that the false humour and bonhomie of the troops was a sign of their apprehension and used the excuse of shaving so that he could be alone with his thoughts. He had nearly finished his shave when the Adjutant entered the dug-out.

'Ah, Melville. That's the ticket—show the Hun that an Englishman's a gentleman even in war.'

Melville attempted to salute with the razor; the Adjutant smiled and waved it away.

'No need for that—we're not in Sandhurst now.'

'No sir—thank you sir.'

Melville knew why the Adjutant was there. It was traditional for officers to leave a final letter for loved ones with their Adjutant if they were about to go on a particularly dangerous mission. Melville had no one he cared for other than Charlotte. They had been writing to one another since the start of their affair using an accommodation address in Nelson Street and a false identity.

The Adjutant seemed ill at ease and told a very poor joke that they both laughed at.

'Don't suppose you'd like me to look after a letter for you?' asked the Adjutant.

'Thank you, sir.' Melville took his hastily written letter from his tunic, which was draped over the back of a chair, and handed it to the older man.

'Just the one, Melville? Young fellow like you—thought you'd have half a dozen.'

'Just one, sir.'

'Well, you never can tell—that friend of yours—Truscott is it? Bit of a dark horse—only gone and given me two. One for the wife and another for some young filly named Daisy.'

'Sorry sir—did you say that Henry's having an *affair?*'

'More of an arrangement—if you know what I mean? She was a dancer at the Hippodrome and he's set her up in a place in Cheapside.'

'He's got a mistress?' Melville found it difficult to disguise his anger.

'Shouldn't have mentioned it. I know you're close to him and I assumed you knew—although I must say I'm not surprised. That wife of his is a bit of a cold fish. That's what comes of marrying for money.'

'She married him for his money?—I didn't realise?'

'No the other way round, dear boy—he married her for *her* money.'

'Oh—I understand.' Melville closed the razor and wiped his face. He muttered under his breath: 'Now I understand—everything.'

'Look, Melville, old chap. Keep it under your hat, would you? I shouldn't really have broken a confidence—brothers in arms and all that.'

Melville assured him that he wouldn't mention it to anyone and the Adjutant was about to continue on his rounds when he paused and asked.

'Melville?—That's an unusual name. Your father wasn't in the Sudan was he?'

'No sir, he was a farmer—but I believe he had a distant cousin in the army.'

'Ah, I knew a Melville once—sound fellow. Do you know you're the absolute spit of him?'

Melville looked at the middle-aged Adjutant and suddenly recognised him from long ago. He remembered a young man—young and idealistic—but the man now before him was old and jaded, the survivor of too many campaigns. The Adjutant made his excuses and left Melville to his thoughts. Melville stared at his Webley in its 'Sam Browne' belt, which lay on the chair. There would be no need for a divorce, he thought—it would only take one bullet and all their problems would be solved. The Adjutant would never realise that his loose tongue had cost Henry his life. Why should he feel guilty about it? He had killed so many what difference would one more make?

Half an hour before daybreak his platoon was in the forward trenches, lined up alongside the ladders, ready to climb out of the trench. The wire in front had been cut to allow them easy access to no-man's land and from there it was only few hundred yards to the German front line. For the past week the cloud cover had been too low for air surveillance and it had been decided that a reconnaissance party would be sent out to assess the strength of the enemy position prior to the main assault.

Melville and his men waited in anxious silence for the order to advance. The men took a last drag of their cigarettes. In the dark, the glow of a cigarette could betray your position to an enemy sniper. It was a cloudy night and little moonlight illuminated the barren landscape. The plan was to cross as close to the enemy trenches as possible, assess the position of the major machine-gun emplacements and, if conditions were favourable, send in a raiding party to capture prisoners to bring back for interrogation. Melville was in a better position than any of the others to assess the German defences due to his superior night vision but what he saw only served to convince him of the suicidal nature of their mission. The enemy was well dug in with heavy machine-gun posts providing complete coverage of no-man's land, making it a perfect killing-field. Their only chance of success or, more realistically, of survival was to cross no-man's land without being detected and to surprise the defenders, and then to get in and out while the enemy were in disarray. He was very pessimistic; he had learned the hard way to respect the Germans. They were well trained and well led; it would take a miracle for any his platoon to return alive.

He checked his wrist watch — five minutes to go — then looked down the trench and wondered how many, of these men would return. He knew from past experience that war was a lottery and the only prize was survival marred by mental or physical scars. Why did he keep on coming back for more? Perhaps it was all he knew?

Two minutes to go; he drew his Webley and cocked the hammer. He could see Henry halfway down the trench. Henry looked up and nodded and Melville nodded back. Once out on no-man's land it would be easy to shoot him. Melville could see clearly in the dark but everyone else would assume a German sniper. But then he paused for thought: once he had fired at Henry, the enemy would be alerted and the British soldiers would all be cut down by German machine-gun fire. He would need to time his shot carefully and to wait until the first shots had been fired — then choose his moment and kill Henry in the confusion of battle.

It was time — he waved and his men climbed silently out of the trench. They advanced slowly fanning out so as to cover as much ground as possible and to make themselves less vulnerable. Henry moved forwards a few yards to Melville's right and about five paces ahead. He would make an easy target from this distance — a single shot — a clean kill.

Now the forward troops were about twenty yards from the German's trench. Melville took careful aim and waited. The second shot fired would be the one that killed Henry. Suddenly the sky exploded in a brilliant light — dazzling Melville's sensitive eyesight — flares! Then heavy machine-guns opened up — they had walked into an ambush.

He threw himself into the mud searching for some cover but found none. The machine-gun bullets cut down the line of men in front of him, whizzed over his head and peppered the ground around him. He looked to his right and saw Henry laying crumpled in the mud. At first he thought that he was dead and felt relieved that the Germans had done his job for him, then he saw Henry move and decided that he would have to finish the job himself before he could attempt to withdraw his men.

Melville crawled and slithered on his belly across the mud until he reached Henry's side. Henry was doubled over clutching his stomach in obvious pain. He coughed and blood came from the corner of his mouth. Melville raised the Webley, then Henry looked up at him and Melville's resolve faded. He lowered his gun.

Henry tried to smile: 'Don't think much of the band.'

Melville laughed. Those were the first words that Henry had ever said to him at that cocktail party when he had met him and Charlotte. His hatred of Henry evaporated and he recognised him as a friend once again. He remembered that first meeting as though it was yesterday—even how he had replied to Henry that day:

'Well—I suppose there is a war on.'

Henry laughed and coughed, blood splattering the mud by his face.

'Tell me is it bad?' asked Henry and moved his arm. Melville saw where a deep wound had been cut through Henry's stomach and chest by the machine-gun bullets.

'Yes—it is.'

'Thought so.' Henry's breathing seemed more laboured. He pulled Melville close until his ear was close to Melville's mouth. He coughed again and Melville felt blood speckle his cheek.

'Look after Charlotte for me—will you?' said Henry. 'Promise me you will.'

Melville promised then held Henry's hand until he died. Melville lay in the mud and cried for a lost friend, one whom he had planned to kill only minutes before. All Henry's sins were washed away and Melville remembered only the friendship, not the betrayal nor the pain. Instead he was seized by a feeling of rage; he picked up the knapsack of hand grenades that Henry had been carrying and ran towards the enemy machine-gun post firing his Webley.

The stretcher bearers recovered Melville from the remains of the German machine-gun post after the counter-attack had consolidated Melville's mad single handed charge. He appeared to be fatally wounded and was taken to a field hospital to die. However they failed to take account of his 'talents' and within a few weeks he was ready to be discharged. His actions had saved the remains of his men and the subsequent counter-attack had taken a considerable section of the enemy line. Melville was saddened to learn that, as well as Henry, over half his company had also died. It was decided that the losses would have been even greater without Melville's selfless and suicidal action and he was consequently awarded the VC.

It was all a long time ago; he had lost his Webley and Charlotte's letters many years ago and the memory of Henry's face had faded — but he still had his VC in the tobacco tin in his wardrobe.

§

The barber finished shaving and the shock of the aftershave jolted Melville out of the past. He paid the barber and left with a clean shave and a clean conscience. Remembering a promise he'd made to Sheryl, he took a detour to the newsagent on the way back to the apartment and bought the evening edition of the *Echo*. He had been home for nearly an hour, when Sheryl arrived clutching more carrier bags.

'Hiya Lee, what do you fancy: saucy red-head, sultry brunette or tah dah!' She pulled on a metallic purple wig.

'- Sci-fi strumpet?'

Melville ignored her and continued reading the paper.

'You made the front page,' he said.

She squealed, jumped on the sofa next to him and snatched the paper from his hand. She read the headline out loud. 'MYSTERY WOMAN ABDUCTED FROM THE ROYAL'

She giggled: 'I like being a *mystery woman*. That's me to a tee—dark and mysterious.'

He looked at her smiling face and purple wig and laughed. She punched him on the arm then continued to read the article.

It was mid-morning a few weeks later. Lee had gone for one of his walks and Sheryl was in the bedroom trying on a new wig she'd had made for herself, an accurate copy of her own hair prior to the fall. There was a knock at the door followed by the sound of a key turning. She checked her watch and adjusted the wig; Michelle wasn't due for another hour.

'Hiya,' Michelle appeared in the doorway with her hoover; she looked harassed. 'Sorry I'm early—I'll come back later if you like.'

'No—it's fine. Fancy a coffee?' Michelle always had a coffee and a chat.

'No thanks luv, gorra rush today. Goin' to see me mam in the 'ome later an' me car's broke down so gorra get two buses.'

Michelle didn't know that her mother was Sheryl's sister, nor that her aunty Shirley, who was in her seventies and supposed to be living in Australia, was in fact standing before her and was a vampire. Since the explosion Sheryl had only been able to keep up to date with her sister's health through her weekly conversations with Michelle.

On the day of the explosion Jean had done what Sheryl had told her to, and had been found by the police playing hide and seek in Lime Street Station. It had been decided by all concerned that she was now a danger to herself and, reluctantly, Michelle had allowed her to be moved to a nursing home.

Sheryl had been unable visit her sister Jean there because the home would probably ask difficult questions. Now she saw an opportunity to see her again.

'Don't worry—I'll give you a lift.'

'I don' wanna put yer to no trouble.'

'No probs, babe. Lee will be gone for ages and I know where he keeps his car keys. You'll have time for that coffee after all.'

A short while later they were sitting in Lee's Range-Rover in the underground car park and Sheryl was having problems starting the car.

'Yer sure about this?' asked Michelle

'Course, no worries,' Sheryl fiddled with the switches. 'I mean how difficult can it be to drive?'

'Wot!—Yer can't drive?'

'Course, babe—but always automatics. Lee won't let me drive this but we'll be back before he knows it. Tell you the truth, I think he's got a bit of OCD—he's always polishing it.'

The engine started and Sheryl slammed it into gear; there was a squeal from the tyres and the car leapt forwards out of the parking space. Michelle held on tight as they narrowly missed a concrete post.

'Sweet Jesus!'

'Said it was dead easy,' Sheryl smiled at her.

'Look where yer goin'!'

They narrowly avoided a parked car.

By the time they reached the nursing home Sheryl had mastered the gears and was feeling rather pleased with herself but Michelle felt as though she'd aged several years. They pulled into the car park.

'Piece of cake,' said Sheryl. She parked next to a small concrete post but forgot to take the car out of gear; when she took her foot of the clutch pedal, the car lurched forward with a sickening crunch. They got out and surveyed the damage. The number plate was cracked.

'He won't notice that,' said Sheryl confidently. Michelle wasn't so sure.

'Don't bother waitin', luv,' said Michelle. 'I'll get the bus back later.'

'I'd like to meet your mum — if you don't mind?'

It seemed ungrateful to refuse after the lift so Michelle reluctantly agreed — and reminded herself to get out her rosary beads for the trip home.

The car park had once been the front garden of a large Victorian house, since converted into the nursing home. They walked to the front porch and rang the bell, after a few moments, the door opened and they were greeted by a nurse and the faint, background smells of stewed cabbage and urine.

The nurse directed them to Jean's room on the first floor. A modern, glass lift had been added to the side of the building but they went up the ornately carved, original staircase and found her sitting in a brightly lit room watching a small, portable TV.

'Hiya mam, how yer doin' today? This is Sheryl, she gave me a lift coz me car's knackered.'

Jean looked up from her programme, acknowledged Michelle — then recognised Sheryl.

'Shirl' where've you been? I woz worried 'bout yer luv.'

'No, Mam, it's Sheryl — not Shirl' ' said Michelle then whispered to Sheryl: 'Sorry — she thinks yer her sister, Shirley.'

'What 'appened to that funny fella?' Jean asked. 'Did yer sort 'im out?'

'She's confused,' Michelle said under her breath, 'Some days are better than others.'

'I 'id like yer told me, sis,' Jean took hold of Sheryl's hand and wouldn't let go, '- but you didn't come for us, did yer? Don't go Shirl, stay forra a cuppa an' a chin wag.'

'No, Mam, let 'er be,' said Michelle.

Jean was getting agitated. Sheryl suggested that she'd keep her company while Michelle went to get some tea. After Michelle had left, Sheryl told Jean how she *was* really Shirley and promised to come back to see her soon if she could keep their 'little secret'. By the time Michelle returned, they were chatting and Jean was calm once again.

'Look after yerself, Mam,' said Michelle once tea was finished. 'See yer Wednesday; shud 'ave me car back by then.'

'Lovely to have met you, Jean,' said Sheryl.

'You too Sheryl,' replied Jean with a wink. 'See yer Wednesday.'

'No Mam, just me — not Sheryl.'

Jean looked agitated again.

'I don't mind,' said Sheryl. 'I'm not doing anything; I can give you a lift — again.'

Michelle went pale at the thought but, to calm her mum down, she agreed to bring Sheryl on the understanding that she'd do the driving. The return journey was, in fact, slightly less terrifying and as long as Michelle looked at her rosary and not at the road she was only aware of the near misses by the sound of car horns.

On Wednesday Michelle collected Sheryl from the apartment block in her resurrected hatchback and drove them both to the nursing home. Jean seemed very pleased to see Sheryl again, in fact she seemed more pleased to see Sheryl than her own daughter. She kept whispering to Sheryl and finding excuses to send Michelle off on one pointless errand after another and every time Michelle returned she could hear them laughing about something, but they immediately changed the subject when she entered the room. Eventually she'd had enough of being ignored and made up an excuse to leave early. She had no intention of bringing Sheryl again and tried to explain why to her mum without upsetting her or offending Sheryl. Unfortunately this backfired somehow and it was decided that Sheryl would come to visit her mum on the days Michelle couldn't make it.

Sheryl and Michelle drove back to Sheryl's apartment in silence. Sheryl lost in thought over something that Jean had said to her in confidence. Was it true? She was curious; Sheryl was always curious but she couldn't just come out and ask Michelle; it was too delicate a subject.

'You and your mum look dead alike,' she said.

'Like two peas in a pod; only difference is the 'air.'

'Wasn't she a red-head too?' (Sheryl already knew that she wasn't.)

'She was dark like the rest of the family; it's only me and Natasha who are carrot tops.'

'Natasha?'

'Me daughter — twenty-two she is an' just finished at Uni. She's the clever clogs of the family, not thick like the rest of us.'

'Did your dad have the red hair then?'

'No — me cousin always teased me. Sed I wuz the milkman's daughter not me dad's.'

'Your dad still alive?'

'Died ten year ago—heart attack. 'Adn't seen him for years though; he didn't really keep in touch after he left us.' Michelle smiled a sad smile. 'Perhaps I wuz the milkman's after all.'

'Does Natasha live nearby?'

'She does now. She was livin' with her bloke but he was a right knob head so she dumped 'im and now me mam's moved out, she's moved back in wiv me.'

'Where are you now?'

'Temporary flat while they repair the block.'

'What happened?'

'Explosion—killed one of the neighbours.'

'Was it gas or something?'

'Don't know, they still 'aven't a clue. Same thing 'appened on the Wirral a few weeks before—killed sum ol' bloke.'

Back at the apartment, Sheryl asked Michelle to come up for a coffee. She wanted more answers to her questions without appearing too nosey, but she'd just poured the coffee when the front door slammed and Melville stormed in,

'Unbelievable!' he shouted then he spotted Michelle.

'Hiya Lee—what's up?' Sheryl asked.

'He's only damaged my car again.'

'Who?'

'Grimes of course—scratched the paint last time. Now he's broken the number plate. Wait until I get my hands on him!'

Sheryl and Michelle looked at one another.

'Perhaps it wasn't him?' said Sheryl.

'Who else could it be? It's been parked there since I waxed it the other day and it wasn't broken then. I'm going to go and see him right now and give him a piece of my mind.'

'Perhaps it was someone else.'

'Who else could it be?'

Michelle decided it was time to go. She made her excuses and slipped away.

The following morning, while she was cleaning another apartment in the block, she decided to pop in to see if Sheryl had sorted things out with Lee. Sheryl opened the door.

'Hiya luv jus -' said Michelle.

Sheryl was wearing a black 'afro' wig.

'D'yer like it?' asked Sheryl.

'Erm — it's *different*.'

'Thought I'd give Lee a surprise when he gets back.'

'How are things?'

'Things? Oh — the car? Fine. He was really arsey for a few hours but I put on the water works and promised never to drive it again, then he was putty in me hands. He's even agreed to give me a lift to see your mum tomorrow.'

'Don't worry, Sheryl. Yer don't need to put yerself to no trouble.'

'Wouldn't miss it for the world hun. I like chatting with your mum and I'm not doing anything tomorrow.'

'Thanks, luv — long as it's no bother. Does her good to see people, an' she likes yer too.'

'You seeing her tonight?'

'No — 'Bingo night'. Our Natasha's goin' after work.'

'Gotta rush babe. Lee'll be back soon and I've still gotta find where he's hiding his car keys.'

'But — I thought you'd promised?'

Sheryl smiled. 'Only said: "cross me heart and hope to die". That doesn't count.'

The following morning Sheryl and Melville drove to the nursing home but, as they parked, Sheryl recognised Michelle's hatchback in the car park.

'That's funny, Lee. Thought she was coming tomorrow.'

'Perhaps we should come back another day?'

'No worries. We won't stay long and you can meet me little sister.'

They rang the bell but when the nurse came to the door and Sheryl asked to see Jean she seemed uncomfortable.

'I'm sorry; I thought you knew?'

'Knew what?'

'I'm afraid she passed away last night.'

Sheryl glanced at Melville then pushed past the nurse. He followed, apologising, as she ran up the stairs then he was spotted by Michelle and another, younger woman who emerged from the matron's office to the left of the front door.

'Hi, Lee. You've 'eard 'ave yer?'

'Yes — sorry — was it sudden?'

'They think it was 'er 'eart or 'er asthma. She was right as rain when Natasha saw her last night.' She nodded to indicate the young red-headed woman beside her, who held her arm and looking tearful.

'Yeah — right as rain,' said the young woman and sniffed.

'Where's Sheryl?' Michelle asked. She looked around and then to Melville for an answer.

He decided to give her some time and replied, 'She's gone to the loo.'

'We're just off to see Father Murphy about the funeral.' Michelle held up a carrier bag. 'Been picking up the last of 'er personal things. Tell Sheryl I'll catch up with 'er next week.'

Sheryl had made it to Jean's room without being noticed by the staff and slipped inside closing the door. The room was bare and all the personal items had already been removed—it seemed almost ready for its next occupant—except that the previous one had yet to vacate the premises. Her sister's body lay under a white sheet and Sheryl, who was used to corpses, went to stand over it. She'd lost count of the number of bodies she'd stood next to over the years. Usually she associated death or a fresh kill with a sense of elation, the yearning for blood about to be satisfied; this time there was no joy only sadness for a lost sister and a lost life.

She turned back the sheet and looked at the familiar face now subtly changed. Jean looked relaxed and at peace, a peace that Sheryl knew that she could never experience. Jean looked as though she was sleeping and, as Sheryl reached out and touched her sister's cheek, she almost expected the eyes to open. The flesh felt cold and waxy and the eyes remained stubbornly closed; she bent and kissed her sister on the forehead. She felt tears welling up in her eyes and dabbed at them with a tissue.

'Glad I put on me waterproof mascara, babe,' she confided. 'Don't want anyone wondering why I'm crying.' She blew her nose and bending close to her sister's ear, whispered: 'Night, night, sleep tight—mind the bugs don't bite.'

All personal items had been cleared from the room, the family photographs and trinkets had been removed, all that remained on the side table was a paperweight. Perhaps it belonged to the nursing home but that didn't matter; it had been with Jean at the end. Sheryl slipped it in her handbag and turned to leave, blowing a final kiss from the door.

Melville sat waiting in the car lost in his memories, when Sheryl bounced into the passenger seat.

'Hiya.'

'You OK?' he asked.

'Fine, babe.'

'Sure?'

'Jeanie's at peace; now we can move on and leave our past behind.'

He started the car and was about to reverse when he noticed that she was holding what appeared to be a large stone in her hand.

'What's that?'

'Think it's a paperweight. Found it in her room and thought I'd take it as a keepsake.' She passed it to Melville.

He turned it over.

'It's not a paperweight—it's a fossil.'

He drove slowly back into the city, as they reached the Strand, she turned to him.

'Lee, I can't go home yet; there's something I need to do.'

Soon they were parked behind the University buildings and Sheryl walked off purposefully, Melville hurrying to keep up.

'Where are you going?' he asked.

'To have a talk to God.'

'Sorry?'

He realised that she was heading in the direction of the Catholic Cathedral, which was just around the corner. They crossed the road and approached a long flight of steps stretching from the pavement to the Cathedral high above. She stopped at the base of the steps.

'You don't have to come Lee. I'm perfectly safe with God—we have an understanding.'

He was puzzled, but sometimes it was best not to ask questions.

'No, I'd like to come—if you don't mind.'

She touched his arm and pointed to the stone staircase.

'Always makes me think of that Led Zeppelin song.'

'Which one?'

'Think about it, Soft lad—which one do you think?'

They both smiled.

'Race you to the top?'

She ran up the steps laughing and Melville followed slowly behind. She didn't seem to be grieving her sister's death as he would have imagined her to. Perhaps this was her way of coping; he decided to keep quiet.

When he joined her the top she was staring up at Cathedral. He had never seen anything like it before, not up close. The building was the shape of a large cone with a stained-glass cupola at the top. It looked more like something from a James Bond film than a house of worship.

'I think it's beautiful—don't you, Lee?' she said.

He was unconvinced but thought it best to say nothing.

'They call it "Paddy's wigwam".'

He looked at it again, half expecting the top to open and a rocket to shoot out.

'It looks like a birthday cake for Jesus,' she added. 'Perhaps that's why God loves us best.'

'Who?—Scousers?'

'No! Catholics—Soft lad; we're the chosen people!'

'I thought that was the Jews?'

'Perhaps God's got several favourites? — like when you have a tin of *Quality Street* at Christmas and everyone's got few favourites, not just the one. Perhaps religions are like that too? God loves us all, even those who worship the toffee finger?'

She touched his arm.

'You stay here — I'll only be a few minutes. Just need to warn God that Jeanie's on her way.'

'I'll come too — if you don't mind?'

Sheryl took his arm and they walked through the automatic door in to the Cathedral. The interior was a large open space, the altar in the centre and the pews arranged around it in a circle. Sunlight streamed through the stained-glass cupola and brightly coloured patches of light illuminated the walls and floor. Around the periphery there were side chapels of various sizes. Sheryl genuflected towards the altar then turned and headed towards a small chapel on the left while Melville made a half-hearted attempt at the sign of the cross. It had been many years since he'd last done that.

She took a votive candle from a tray.

'Pop a quid in the box will you, Lee?'

'I haven't got one.'

'What is it with you and shrapnel? You'll have to put in a fiver.'

Melville placed a note in the collection box and took a second candle for himself. Sheryl lit hers and placed it on the stand and he did the same.

'Thanks, Lee — Jeanie will appreciate that.'

He said nothing; he'd lit the candle for someone else.

He left her to pray, walked outside onto the large paved area that surrounding the building and sat on the top step looking out over Liverpool. A few minutes later she sat on the step alongside him.

'All done and dusted. God's had a word with St Peter to keep an eye out for Jean Malone.'

'Do you really believe in God?'

'Course I do.'

'Why?'

'You've got to believe in something. Why not God?'

'Heaven and Hell—angels—everything?'

'You either believe in everything or nothing; doesn't make sense otherwise.'

'Aren't you worried then? Worried about Hell?'

'Why should I be? God and I have got an understanding, like I said. He knows I don't mean any harm.'

'But you kill people—lots and lots of people.'

'I know I do, but it's nothing personal. It's the way I am—and the way God made me. He made me a vampire.'

'I thought your "Billy Fury" did that?'

'It was all God's doing, Lee. Doesn't matter who did it; God knew it was going to happen.'

'So God turns a blind eye to you killing people?'

'I think he looks at me like we used to look at our cat, Monty. He was a lovely cat, good-natured, always purring or sitting on your knee for a cuddle, never scratched or bit anyone—ever. But every day he'd go hunting and kill some poor blackbird or mouse. But we could never get angry with him because he was too lovable.'

'You think you're God's pet?'

'I think he looks down and says to himself: "There she

42

goes again, that Sheryl Malone—killed another. How many is that so far this year, St Peter?" He knows I can't help it; it's how I was made—how *God* made me.'

'You don't feel guilty?'

'Why?—I think guilt's overrated. What's the point of crying over spilled blood? People die every day from traffic accidents or cancer. Everyone dies eventually—except us of course. The worst you could say about me is that I'm speeding things up for them.'

'So you come here when you kill someone?'

'No but I come here lots, just for a chat most of the time.'

'When?'

'When you think I'm shopping. Don't you ever wonder why I never buy anything?'

'Why didn't you tell me?'

'You never tell me where you go on your walks do you? You're dead mysterious about that; have you got a wife and six kids tucked away in Toxteth?'

Melville laughed and Sheryl smiled.

'What do you talk about with God?' he asked.

'Lots of different things. We've even talked about you.'

'What did God say about me?' He put his arm around her shoulder.

'He said Lee Melville's a good man.'

'Am I?'

'Course Lee, God's never wrong—there were just a few things he mentioned. He said you need to lighten up, enjoy yourself, and stop feeling guilty about everything. And you need to remember to put the top back on the toothpaste tube.'

'That all?'

'Just about. Let's go out tonight, Lee—and you can practice enjoying yourself.'

'Suppose I've no option if God said so.'

'Well he moves in mysterious way—bit like me Uncle Bobby on the dance floor after a few bevvies.'

They walked down the stairs arm in arm.

'Why don't we go to that charity ball next week?' she suggested.

'Which ball?'

'The fancy dress one.'

'No—I don't do fancy dress.'

'Lighten up Lee—God said so. It'll be fun.'

'It won't be; it'll be embarrassing.'

'At least think about it. I've got a great idea for our costumes.'

'No and no again—don't you listen?'

'Not when I'm doing God's work I don't. We'll talk about it later—when you've changed your mind.'

ABERCROMBY SQUARE

Peter had just finished dissecting the last of the mice that he'd euthanased that morning. Wasn't that a typically British way of disguising the truth, he thought: 'euthanase' sounded so much nicer than 'killed' even though the result for the mice was the same. He packaged up the last of the tissue samples; he intended to send some to the histology department at the University to see if they could detect any abnormal changes in the cells. The others he'd send to his friend at the Royal to see if toxicology could explain what had happened to the mice.

Back to square one again. This batch had seemed so promising but you never knew what could happen when you moved on to animal experiments. The DNA result had looked promising — and much better than results from the previous eleven trials. He'd thought he was really on to something and even his professor had been enthusiastic enough to agree to the extra funding, but after this setback his PhD now looked less certain. He'd probably still get it awarded but it wouldn't be the sort of unqualified success that would guarantee him a permanent research post. The department was always fighting with the others at the University for funding, and a discovery that would be headline news would have secured its budget for the foreseeable future — and Peter his job.

He cleared away the remains of the mice and checked his watch. It was still over an hour until lunch. He often felt hungry after euthanasia, probably something to do with the limbic system in the brain, he thought, the area concerned with primal urges such as hunger and sex. He'd killed something so his brain was telling him to eat. Perhaps he'd have an early lunch and give in to his primal urge. He smiled and regretted that this was the only primal urge he'd have any chance of satisfying that day.

Fifteen minutes later he was sitting on a bench in Abercromby Square eating a prawn sandwich from the student cafeteria although, after the second mouthful, he decided that mouse sandwich would probably have been more palatable. He finished it reluctantly, washed down with a warm can of Cola. He'd be in the lab for the rest of the afternoon writing up the result of the trial and wouldn't get back to his room until late that night because he'd promised to pop over to see Michelle's new flat on his way home. With this in mind, and because it was quite sunny and the hedge around the garden sheltered him from the wind, he decided to stay in the Square for the remainder of his lunch hour.

But, although he tried to clear his mind and enjoy the sun, he kept thinking about the failed trial. He still couldn't understand what had gone wrong with the mice. They'd all been fit and healthy at first, a dozen pristine, white mice with beady, red eyes and they'd been in a large communal cage to allow them to socialise and feed freely. He'd kept them for a week beforehand, recording their weight and making sure that they were healthy before the trial began.

Then he'd inoculated them with the new batch of retro virus. At first nothing had happened then they began to become aggressive towards one another. Initially the fights were over food, little scuffles more out of irritation than malice but, over the next few days, the attacks became prolonged and vicious, and occasionally severe enough to draw blood. On the morning of the fifth day he had found one of the mice dead. Usually he would have put this down to natural causes but the other mice had begun to eat the corpse, which was strange. He'd removed the remains of the mouse and narrowly avoided being bitten by one of the others. From then on, he separated them into individual cages and used thick gloves when handling them. He had expected them to become placid once again, now they were isolated from one another but, in fact, they continued to grow more aggressive, their consumption of food initially increased and they all became more muscular. The growth in aggression and musculature lasted about a week and then they all began to lose interest in the food and, by the end of the second week, they had stopped eating completely. Whatever he fed them they would ignore and gradually, week by week, they lost weight and became more and more lethargic. However none of them died. At the end of the month, he decided to stop the trial and euthanase the survivors in order to discover if a post mortem would determine a cause of their bizarre behaviour.

Peter closed his eyes and enjoyed the feel of the sun on his face. He remembered happier times in these gardens. When they were undergraduates, he and Rachel used to meet there most lunchtimes; she was studying English and he Biology. People had thought they made a strange couple;

she was a larger than life and always ready to voice her opinions, and he was quiet and studious. Neither impression was entirely accurate; Rachel was feisty and opinionated but deeply insecure requiring constant reassurance, while Peter was quietly confident in his own abilities. He had cultivated his air of slight detachment as a way of concealing his intelligence and cynicism.

Peter had been perfecting this disguise over many years. After Paul's murder there had been much anger and recrimination between his parents although he still didn't understand why. Eventually they had divorced and he had moved with his mother to be near to her family in Wales. A new school had brought new challenges and a new curriculum had meant that he had to repeat a year of his GCSE course. He was tall and gangly with a strange accent and NHS spectacles and that guaranteed that he would be bullied. However, because he was taller and a year older than the bullies, they didn't risk anything physical. Also, by pretending to be unaware of their cruel jokes at his expense, he was often able to defuse unpleasant situations and they didn't consider him a threat. Surprisingly this naïve, innocent act was attractive to the opposite sex; it brought out a latent maternal instinct in the most unlikely of women.

By the time Peter arrived at University he no longer had to play the part; he'd become it. The NHS spectacles had given way to contact lenses but the floppy unkempt hair remained, as did the nerdish obsessions. It was due to one such obsession that he met Rachel. In his second term, he helped organise a Sci-fi convention at the Student Union. He was collecting the entrance fees at the door with his friend and fellow nerd, Ben. Peter was dressed as a Vulcan from Star Trek with painted on eye brows and false pointed ears while Ben was dressed as Dr Who. Rachel appeared from nowhere, a whirlwind of multi-coloured scarves and rattling jewellery accompanied by a pale youth clutching a bulky video camera.

She was reporting on the Sci-fi convention for the student on-line magazine. She thrust a microphone into Peter's face and began asking him questions while the youth beside her struggled to focus the camera. Peter tried to explain that the convention was a serious affair and not a laughing matter when one of his ears fell off. The resulting video was an internet hit and made Rachel and Peter unlikely celebrities on the campus.

Although Rachel enjoyed the praise, she had a sneaking feeling that she'd exploited the good nature of her 'Vulcan' and decided to track him down and apologise. Peter reassured her that he hadn't taken offence and that he saw the funny side. She was relieved and suggested a drink to thank him for being so understanding. She decided not to go to the student bar, which was much too public and she didn't want people to get the wrong idea. After all she was a bohemian and very hip and Peter — well, he was a nerd. They walked and talked until they reached a small pub on the way to Rachel's flat. The Belvedere was tiny and tucked in a side street. She discovered that he was interesting and charming and, as the alcohol flowed, she decided that he actually looked quite attractive in a geeky sort of way. He just seemed a bit helpless. She reached over and tucked his collar in. Drinks led to an Indian restaurant — and back to her flat.

That had been eight years ago. If Peter kept his eyes tight shut he could almost hear her voice and smell her perfume, a heavy scent that always seemed to linger in a room after she had left, like the tail of a shooting star. For the first few months after her death he'd kept a bottle and would spray it in the flat and then pretend that she was in another room. But after his strange pigeon dream, he'd never felt the need again. Rachel was dead and, like the mice, she wouldn't be coming back. He stared rather sadly across Abercromby Square. He knew that he needed to start again but, unfortunately, life was more difficult to arrange than a medical trial. He threw the last of his lunch in a bin and returned to the Department to write up his notes.

That evening he arrived at the address he'd been given by Michelle, which was on the other side of town and was part of a large council estate. She'd been moved there after the explosion as a temporary measure by the council until her old flat could be repaired. Unfortunately for Peter, because he had rented off a private landlord he had not been rehomed and had had to make his own arrangements. The tenants in his old apartment in Cheapside still had a few months left on their lease but luckily the University took pity on him and allowed him to rent a college room that had become available after a foreign student dropped out.

The room wasn't ideal for someone of his age. It was small with a single bed, a small desk, a tiny *en-suite* bathroom and with a view over the wheelie bins. He was surrounded by young undergraduates, who spent most of their time either drunk or practicing procreation. His nights were punctuated by rugby songs or squeaking bed springs and he felt prematurely old and lonely. The room was so tiny and Spartan that the only personal item he'd brought with him was his IKEA rug and even that was frustrating because he still didn't know what it was called. Peter often joked that everything in IKEA was named after a James Bond villain or a character from Lord of the Rings; unfortunately someone, probably Rachel, had cut the tag off the back.

He parked his car under a street lamp and after checking the address got out, crossed to the lifts and pressed the button. The block of flats was scruffy compared to the one he'd shared with Michelle prior to the explosion. After waiting for a few minutes for a lift to arrive he realised that it was probably broken and took the stairs to the tenth floor. By the time he arrived at Michelle's door, he was hot and dishevelled from the climb. The bunch of flowers he'd bought had got trapped in the fire door on the sixth floor and he was worried that the chocolates might have melted, as they were tucked under his sweaty armpit.

He'd decided on flowers and chocolates rather than his customary choice of wine because he didn't know what sort of occasion this was meant to be. Michelle had casually asked him the week before if he'd like to come over one evening to see her new flat and to have something to eat. He'd readily agreed: anything to escape from his undergraduate Hell for a few hours.

He knew that he was invited for a meal but wasn't sure how smartly he should dress. That was something he was generally undecided about. Although there wasn't an official uniform in the department there was an unofficial understanding about was appropriate for each grade of researcher. An undergraduate, would be expected to wear college sweat shirts or a band t-shirt and the choice of band had to be suitable, either heavy-metal or punk. Postgraduates should wear the classic check shirt and sweater combo and for the senior researchers a sports jacket replaced the sweater and the shirt had a button-down collar. Finally a professor should wear a tweed jacket with elbow patches and a bow tie. Peter presently hovered between the sweater and sports jacket. If he wore the jacket too early he would be considered too cocky and that might hinder his chances of promotion—but if he left it too long they might consider him immature and that might be detrimental too.

Tonight, in desperation, he was wearing both the sweater and the sports jacket and that coupled with the climb up the stairs caused by the broken lift was the reason for his flushed appearance when Michelle opened the door.

'Sweet Jesus—what's 'appened to yer, luv?'

'Sorry?'

'Did they mug yer—them scallies?'

'Oh, no—just a bit hot; the lift's not working.'

'Come in luv.' Michelle took the crushed flowers with a questioning look.

'They got trapped in a fire door.'

He handed over the squashed box of chocolates.

'I dropped these as well, sorry.'

'It's the thought that counts, luv. Sit yerself down; tea's nearly ready.'

Peter sat on a threadbare sofa. The room was small and the furniture mismatched. The walls were painted in red, yellow and green.

'Previous tenants were Rastas,' Michelle explained from the kitchen. 'Hardly seem worth paintin' as its only temporary. They say we'll be back in the flats in a month or so.'

'What happened to your furniture?'

'Got lost in the fire. The insurance will pay up — eventually like, so 'm gonna wait till we get back 'ome. Got the sofa from a friend and the other stuff from a charity to tide us over.'

Peter looked around. The furniture was a haphazard collection of different ages and styles rather like a kitsch V&A collection. In one corner stood a large TV and in the other what appeared to be a birdcage on a stand, covered by a grey cover.

'Sorry?' said Peter, '- you said us?'

'Didn't I tell yer, luv? Me daughter Natasha's moved back in with me. She's split up with 'er fella and I was feelin' a bit lonely with me mam in the care home and not knowin' no one 'ere.'

Michelle came out of the kitchen wiping her hands on a tea towel.

'Tea or coffee, luv? Or would you like a beer?'

'Tea would be lovely.'

They were halfway through their second cup when he heard a key turning in the lock.

'That'll be our Natasha.' Michelle checked her watch. 'She must 'ave missed 'er train.'

A young woman entered. She was probably early twenties, thought Peter, quite pretty with bright, red hair pulled back in a ponytail. She had fair skin, freckles on her nose and wore a thick, black coat. When she took off the coat there was a nurse's uniform underneath.

'Say Hello to Peter,' said Michelle from the kitchen, "e's come for is tea — d'yer remember I said this mornin'?'

'Hiya — sorry, I forgot.' She hung up her coat and, smiling, walked past Peter to remove the cover of the bird cage. There was a flurry of green feathers and a squawk from the bedraggled parrot inside.

'Evenin' Cap'n,' said Natasha.

'Pieces of eight,' replied the parrot, bouncing up and down on its perch. 'Cap'n wantz eez grog — wantz eez grog.'

'Feed 'im Natasha 'es doin' me 'ead in with all 'is sqwarkin'.'

Natasha turned to Peter.

'Meet Captain Morgan,' she said. 'He used to belong to an old Mersey ferry Captain but he's had to go in a home, so we're looking after him now.'

'Is he named after the pirate, Captain Morgan?'

'No?' Natasha looked puzzled, 'He's named after the rum; he won't drink anything else.'

'You give him *rum*?'

'Only the best for the Captain.' Natasha stroked the bird under its chin.

'You sure it won't do him any harm?' Could birds metabolise alcohol?

'He's been drinking it for years apparently, and he gets really arsey if you don't give it to him.'

She filled the parrot's food container with monkey nuts and added a splash of rum to his water bowl. It cracked open a nut, dunked it in the water and swallowed it, eying Peter suspiciously as if he was after its rum. Michelle returned from the kitchen.

'Natasha's always bringin' in waifs and strays, ever since she woz a kid. A cat with one eye, cross-eyed goldfish that sorta thing. She'll make a good mam one day.'

'Mum!' said Natasha, 'I'm sure Peter isn't interested in that.'

She sat on the sofa next to him. He looked quite cute she thought, a bit scruffy perhaps, but now she remembered her mum had said he was a widower so that was probably the reason. She reached out and tucked in his collar that was sticking up.

'Thanks.' Peter was slightly unnerved.

'You looked a bit … untidy.' She smiled then called to Michelle 'What's for tea, Mum I'm starving.'

Michelle carried a large casserole dish from the oven and placed it in the middle of the table.

'Scouse made to the Malone family recipe.' She spooned a ladle full into each bowl. 'Come 'an sit yerselves down before it gets cold.'

The meal was delicious and the company friendly; the conversation ranged from films and books to music. Peter was surprised how much he had in common with Natasha. By the end of the evening he felt as if he'd known her for years. Michelle let them talk. She could see that Natasha was interested in Peter and why not, he was a nice lad, not a knob head like her ex. She cleared away the bowls and piled them in the sink; she'd wash them after Peter left. Then she looked at the wall clock and, wiping her hands on the tea towel, switched on the TV.

'Yer don't mind if I watch *Corrie* do you?'

'Sorry,' said Peter, 'I didn't realise it was so late. I'd better be going.'

He stood up and Natasha smiled and said: 'I'll walk you to your car. Don't want you getting into any trouble.'

They walked down the stairs and across the open space between the tower blocks towards his car. They were deep in conversation and didn't see the man approaching on the BMX bike until he was alongside them.

'Hi, sexy, why don't yer tell this wanker to fuck off an' get yerself a real man?'

'Ignore him and keep walking,' Natasha whispered.

The man stood up on the pedals of the bike and slowly circled them. He suddenly pedalled hard and cut in front, making them jump back out of his path. They paused then continued walking.

'Yer new 'ere, aren't yer ?' The man continued to circle them. 'Yer betta be nice to me if yer know wot's good for yer.'

He pulled up directly in front of them blocking their way. Peter stepped in front of Natasha, but she pushed him out of the way and stood between him and the man on the bike. She was a least a foot shorter than Peter and he could stare over the top of her head at the other man who was probably late teens or early twenties, with close-cropped hair and dressed entirely in black with a baseball cap and a hoodie. The top of a tattoo covered his exposed neck. He leaned on the handlebars and leered at Natasha.

'Why?' said Natasha.

'Or yer cud get 'urt,' said the man.

What happened next happened very quickly; Natasha dropped slightly and her right hand shot out, the palm held upright, while she made a 'ah-uh!' sound. The hand made contact with the man's chin and he toppled backwards to land with a sickening crunch on the tarmac. She stepped over and untangled his legs from the frame of the bike, then rolled him on his side and put him in the recovery position.

'Don't want him choking on his tongue,' she explained.

'That was amazing,' said Peter. 'I mean how? What did you do?'

'Taekwondo. You'd better be on your way before he wakes up.' Natasha took his arm and they walked away from the unconscious man.

'But what about you?'

Natasha gave him what could best be described as a withering look. At Peter's car, they exchanged phone numbers and agreed to meet again. They were standing next to the car when she stood on her tip toes and reached up. Peter thought she was trying to kiss him so he bent down, closed his eyes and pursed his lips. She laughed and tucked his collar in again. He felt embarrassed, got into the car and wound down the window.

'Thanks, you know for erm … everything.' He nodded towards the man.

'No problem.' She smiled, then leaned in through the window and kissed him. 'Now clear off before any more scallies turn up.'

She waved as he drove off and then returned to the unconscious man who was moaning and beginning to regain consciousness. Searching his pockets, she found a wallet containing a few pounds and a bank card in the name of Lewis O'Reilly. She put the wallet back in his pocket, checked he was recovering and then let the air out of his tyres.

Peter had arranged to meet up with his old University friend and fellow 'nerd' Ben the following night. Ben's wife Hannah was on a 'girl's night out' with her friends, giving the two men the opportunity to indulge in their joint passions for Sci-fi and gaming without suffering disparaging comments.

Peter parked his Peugeot in Bixteth Street around the corner from Ben's flat. He looked forward to catching up with Ben's news because they hadn't seen one another for several months. The meeting had come about because he'd phoned Ben the previous week to ask if Ben could have a look at his research notes; a fresh mind might see any obvious flaws in his methods. Ben had suggested that he come over for a few beers and tempted him with a new game: 'Zombie Hotel 3'.

An hour later they'd drunk some beer and finished their pizzas. Peter raised the subject of his research.

'Did you get a chance to have a look at the notes yet, Ben?'

'Yeah, and I don't see what the problem is.' Ben opened two beers and passed one over.

'Instead of increasing their life expectancy, they became *psycho mice* then died. That's the problem.'

'So you didn't manage to stabilise the telomeres?'

'That's the strange bit. When I analysed the DNA — it confirmed that I *had* stabilised the telomeres — but they still died. First of all they ate normally and put on weight and muscle, then stopped eating and withered away.'

'How long did they live? Was it much less than normal?'

'A lot less; I cut the trial short and euthanased them.'

'Killed you mean.' Ben sipped his beer. 'You scientists use jargon to disguise the facts.'

'Unlike lawyers?'

'Touché — but if you *killed* them then you don't know how long they would have lived if you hadn't. Just because they were skinny doesn't mean that they'd have died — you know, like those Tibetan monks who live for years and years on next to nothing.'

'Perhaps it's an absorption thing? I changed their DNA so they needed something else in their diet to make up for some deficiency in their metabolism.'

'Enough of work; how about blitzing a few zombies?' Ben leaned over and switched on the console.'

Two hours later they'd finished off all the beers and the zombies. They'd debated the relative merits of an Uzi sub-machine-gun or pump action shotgun when dealing with the undead and then moved on to the shots.

The following morning Peter woke up on the sofa, an empty bottle of tequila cradled in his arms. He'd had a restless night pursued by Uzi-wielding psycho mice and he now seemed to be suffering his own personal revenge of the zombies. Ben shuffled into the lounge looking so much like one of the undead that Peter momentarily went to reach for his Uzi.

'Mornin', Pete. Feel as shit as me?'

Peter tried to sit up, changed his mind and answered with a groan.

'Thought so — I'll put some coffee on.'

Breakfast of painkillers was washed down with two pints of water and a black coffee but it had little effect. Peter was almost certainly over the alcohol limit so he wouldn't be driving any time soon. They decided that a cooked breakfast would set them on the road to recovery and walked slowly into the city centre.

'Why did you decide to do your PhD on this mice thing?'

'Seemed a good idea; if we can find a way to stabilise the telomeres then it just may help kids with Progenia.'

'Pro- what?'

'Progenia: it's that one were you age really quickly. You get these poor kids who are only ten but look sixty. They don't develop properly and die really young.'

'Are there many of them?'

'Thankfully no — perhaps only a hundred or so in the whole world.'

'So that's why the department was so keen?'

Peter laughed. 'If it works it'll be much bigger than that.'

'Why?'

'If it works it could make us all immortal. That's why the Department were so keen.'

'But — it won't work will it? That's just Sci-fi isn't it?'

'I may already have created some immortal, psycho mice.'

They both laughed.

'Remember me when you're famous, Doctor Frankenstein.'

'He only brought the dead back to life; he never made them immortal.'

'Whatever you say, Pete — but I prefer my zombies in a game'

They walked across Dale Street to a busy restaurant that served American-style breakfasts. A short while later they were feeling slightly better after a large plate of waffles each and two coffees.

'So, if it's going to be so easy to make everyone immortal,' said Ben pushing his plate to one side, 'how come no one's done it before and how come there's only you working on it in the department?'

'Number one—it isn't going to be that easy. There are always downsides, unless you want immortal, psycho mice or something.'

'And that would definitely hurt mouse-trap sales,' Ben said with a smile.

Peter ignored him and continued, 'The department don't want to get fully involved until they're sure it's worth pursuing. Funding is always a problem and they don't want another PR disaster.'

'Oh yeah, I remember now- a couple of years ago—didn't someone claim to have found the cure for baldness?'

'That's right, Jim Carver. He was a junior researcher who had some promising results with a trial, then he found out they weren't going to re-new his contract so he tinkered with the results to make them more impressive and leaked it to the press. It was front page news in one of the nationals. The University got involved and they forced the department to keep Carver on and let him continue the trials. Everything went well until the primate trials; they gave it to the chimps and all their hair fell out.'

Ben laughed; Peter didn't.

'Cue lots of red faces,' Peter continued. 'The Prof got a bollocking from the University for making them look stupid, and Carver got sacked for falsifying results—then the department got their budget cut.'

'But I still don't understand: if it's got potential why are only you are working on it?'

'I was coming to that—that was number two. Lots of other research departments all over the world are working on this but I'm trying a different approach to stabilising the telomeres.'

'How come?'

'It's all due to Obi Wan Kenobi.'

'Of course, you should have told me before! It's not Sci-fi it's all due to the teaching of a fictional Jedi knight, of course it is!'

'Do you remember that first-generation, Star Wars figure of Obi Wan Kenobi that I got on E-bay?'

'The one worth $400 Dollars that you bought for 99p? I think you may have mentioned it before.' Ben yawned theatrically.

'It was because of that. It was misspelled and listed in the wrong category so no one else noticed it; it was listed as 'STARS WAR' figure so it didn't come up in the normal searches, and the advertiser didn't realise how rare it was. I was the only one who spotted it and that was by accident. I'd had a bit to drink and wasn't wearing my contact lenses so I mistyped my search and it came up.'

'So a plastic toy holds the key to immortality?'

'I was doing a search of all the literature on telomers prior to starting my PhD project, dozens of papers from all over the world, all doing the same things, using the same methods and all getting nowhere.'

'And?'

'I thought about old Obi, and altered the search parameters, altered the spellings and looked at papers to do with other genetic abnormalities — and I found it.'

'Found what?'

'An obscure Chinese paper from the 1990's on chromosome mapping. Things have moved on a long way since then and we use different techniques now, but they had some unusual results when they used culture mediums at different Phs.'

'In English please.'

'They thought the results were experimental error but with hindsight I could see that they'd stabilised the telomeres without realising what they'd done.'

'Twenty years ago? Why hadn't anyone else spotted it?'

'The person who translated the paper into English had misspelled its title and the researchers weren't working on telomeres anyway.'

'And now you're using their technique?'

'Well, a development of it. Until I know it works I don't want anyone else claiming the credit; that's why I'm working on my own. Only the Prof knows roughly what I'm doing and he's happy to leave me alone for the time being, until there's something tangible.'

'He doesn't want egg on his face again?'

'Talking of eggs Ben, — are you still hungry?'

Peter felt excited but also puzzled. The thirteenth trial was going well; the mice were still alive and the toxicology results from the mice in the previous trial had pointed to some vitamin deficiencies. He'd tried giving vitamin supplements to the new batch of mice, but for some reason they now seemed unable to absorb them. It was as though the virus had altered their metabolism together with their telomeres. There must be something missing from their diet which would explain the lethargy, all he need to do was find out what. It was just a matter of trial and error.

Early DNA results from the mice and for those of the previous trial showed that the telomeres had been stabilised. Perhaps he'd already managed to create immortal mice. Their aggressive behaviour was a problem but, that might be partially due to the problems with their metabolism, if that could be controlled or eradicated then it might be possible to get approval for primate trials. The department would be understandably cautious no doubt; bald chimps had been a PR disaster. But that would be nothing compared to immortal psycho chimps. Peter smiled as he imagined the tabloid headlines: '*PLANET OF THE SCOUSE APES*'.

He packed away his things and switched off the light in the lab. He was meeting Natasha for a quick drink prior to doing his night shift at the apartment block on Liverpool-One, and he needed to change into his uniform first. If his trial worked out it would guarantee his funding and he would be able to give up his part-time job as a concierge. For now, he was keeping his options open and doing the occasional extra shift providing holiday cover in order to save for a new car. As he walked through the campus he saw the undergraduates collecting for the University Rag Mag. They were in fancy dress. A collection of 'naughty nurses' wheeled a patient covered in bandages past him in a wheelchair. As he walked through Abercromby Square, he was accosted by the Wolfman and Count Dracula.

'Your money or your blood!' said Dracula thrusting a magazine under his nose.

Peter smiled and paid up. He remembered doing this with Rachel years ago; he'd been dressed in his Vulcan outfit complete with ears and she'd been dressed as the Queen Victoria. He was walking back to his room flicking through the rag mag and reminiscing to himself, when a thought suddenly occurred.

'No surely not?' he almost laughed out loud. 'It couldn't be as simple as that—could it?'

He stopped and sat on a wall, deep in thought. What a ludicrous idea—but the more he thought about it, the more sense it made. The mice in trial twelve grew stronger and more aggressive after they had killed the other mouse, then, when they were isolated from one another, they grew weaker and more lethargic. What they needed was—blood! He smiled; he'd been wrong all along. He thought he'd created immortal psycho mice, but it was much simpler than that; they were *vampire* mice—and all he needed to do to prove his hypotheses was to see if blood cured their metabolic problems, that and convince the department that he wasn't insane. Peter laughed out loud and thought of a new headline, *'COUNT CHIMPULA'*

He checked his watch. If he didn't hurry he'd be late for Natasha and she'd give him one of her withering looks, and he'd prefer to deal with vampire chimps rather than one of those. Although they'd only known one another for a few weeks he was old enough to realise already that this was not some casual relationship; it was many years since he last felt so strongly about another human being. Their friendship had quickly gone from lust to love and he now found it difficult to imagine a future without her. Natasha was different from Rachel in almost every way and perhaps that was why he believed that their love was genuine and not some attempt by him to relive his past.

Thirty minutes later Peter had changed and was waiting for her in a bar on Chavasse Park. He sipped a soft drink and had a large glass of white wine waiting for her. He checked his watch—she was late for once. He saw her by the door and waved and she waved back and pushed her way through the crowd.

'Hiya Pete.' She kissed him, sat down at the seat he'd saved for her and took a large gulp from the wine glass.

'Busy day?'

She shrugged, 'Always the same — how are the psycho mice?'

'They might be vampires.'

'I shouldn't have asked — you been at the magic mushrooms again?'

'They really could be vampires.'

'Whatever, — how long have we got?'

Peter checked his watch. 'Ten minutes.'

She handed him her empty glass. 'Same again. I've got to visit my nutty nan this evening -Mum's off to the bingo.'

'As bad as that?'

'You know I love her but she's completely doodle-alley. She thinks her sister from Australia visits her when we're not there. It's all she talks about: Shirley this and Shirley that. She's driving me mum round the bend — she even thinks one of me mum's clients *is* Shirley.'

The second glass seemed to do the trick and Natasha's mood improved so that by the time they were walking through the park, she was looking forward to the visit. She left Peter at the main entrance and walked the short distance to James Street Station.

The night on concierge duty passed slowly. Peter began by writing up his notes, then read the newspaper and then a paperback he found in the back room. He had a few messages from Natasha and arranged to see her again the next evening. At last the night was over and at 7am Phil took over. After coffee and a chat, Peter walked through the city centre and up the hill towards his room. He wasn't working at the Department that day and meant to get a few hours' sleep before meeting up with Natasha. He'd just reached Abercromby Square when his mobile rang, it was Natasha. He knew by her tone that something was up.

'Pete?'

'Hi Tash — you OK?'

'Pete — me nan's dead.'

'Where are you?'

'At home with me mum.'

'Wait there — I'll be right over.'

Within a few days things were organised. The Church and Father Murphy had been booked for ten days' time, the flowers had been ordered and the wake arranged. There was nothing left to do and so Natasha had persuaded her mum to take a short break with an old girlfriend to take her mind off the funeral.

Peter moved in with Natasha while her mum was away and promised to take some time off from his trial so that they could have time together. The weather forecast was good and Natasha seized on a casual remark by him about it being picnic weather and soon she was making sandwiches and they had agreed to take the following day off. The trial was going well and he needed to check on something first thing, and so it was decided that they would quickly pop into the lab on the way.

Next morning they parked the Peugeot around the corner from the lab. There was no need for Natasha to come in but she was curious to see where he worked, and, it being a weekend, there was no senior member of staff around to object. Peter swiped his security card and opened the door.

Natasha had expected it to be a short visit but as the minutes ticked by and Peter sorted through his notes in the office she became restless.

'Come on Pete,' she said. 'You said you'd take the day off.'

'OK Tash, give me five minutes to clear things away and make some notes,' he picked up a folder and disappeared through the door into the main lab beyond.

Natasha checked her watch; she was bored and hungry. She rummaged through the carrier bags containing their picnic, opened a plastic tub and took out a cheese-and-tomato sandwich, took a bite and went looking for Peter.

The lab was a brightly lit room with a long bench down the centre and walls lined with testing apparatus, glass cabinets and computer terminals. It was silent because it was a Saturday morning and the lab was empty. At the far end there was a door marked 'Animal room'. Since there was no sign of Peter in the main lab, she walked the length of the lab, pushed open the door and entered. Inside were racks of cages of all sizes. Two large cages by the door were empty and a pair of thick, gardening gloves lay on top of one of them. The other cages were much smaller and all contained white mice, each cages containing one mouse, a food bowl with pellets in it and a water container. They were all identical except for a coloured tag and a number clipped to the bars. She leaned over the first cage and the mouse inside stood on its hind legs and looked at her, twitching its whiskers.

'Hiya—I used to have a mouse like you, called Derek. What's your name?' She took a piece of cheese from her sandwich and pushed it through the bars. 'Red Leicester—much nicer than those pellets.'

The mouse sniffed the cheese but didn't touch it.

'How about some tomato then?'

She pushed the tomato through the bars.

'Oww!' she snatched her hand back and looked at her finger.

'No need to be so arsey — I'm not trying to steal your pellets.'

She went back into the lab to look for Peter. He burst in through a side door.

'There you are.' He started switching off the lights. 'Where have you been?'

'Looking for you.' She swallowed the last of her sandwich, 'You ready now?'

'Yes.'

'About time too. Look, I've had an idea — let's take the train. I've brought some wine and we can both have a drink. We can pick up the car in the morning — what do you think?'

'OK — where are we going?'

'Wait and see.'

They left the lab and as they passed Peter's car heading down the hill into the city centre a man got out of a 4X4 and followed them. They took a train from Central Station two stops South. As they left the train at St Michael's Station, the man followed them onto the platform and made a call on his mobile.

Leaving the Station she turned right, Natasha led Peter down a steep path into a wooded area. It was as short walk through the trees to a main road. On the other side of the road there was a gate and a sign, 'Festival Park'.

They had their picnic on wooden decking next to a pond in the shade of a Japanese summerhouse. The Japanese

Garden was tucked away behind some tall shrubs a little way from the large lake. Although it was a sunny day this part of the park was deserted. Natasha took off her shoes and dangled her feet in the small, ornamental pond.

'I often come here; it's dead peaceful.' She stretched out her legs. 'You could really believe you were in Japan if some scally hadn't written 'Gerrard for Pope' with the ornamental gravel.'

'I didn't know there was a park here.' Peter sipped his wine.

'It's what's left of the International Garden Festival.'

'When was that?'

'1984 — before we were born, but me mum came here as a kid with me nan, and she always talked about it when I was growing up.'

'You came here as a child then?'

'No, after the festival finished the council closed it and let it rot. When I was little it was boarded up and no one dared come in; it was full of druggies and scallies.'

'So this is all new?' Peter waved around a hand with a chicken drum stick in it.

'Few years ago they restored some bits of the old site. The rest of the land is going to be houses when they can raise the money.'

'What was the festival like?'

'Lots of plants I suppose, but me mum only remembered the slide and the playground. She used to tell me all about it when we came for a walk by the river. Money was tight when I was little and a walk along the prom was a cheap day out. Mum was a single mum and me nan didn't have much neither. We used to come here a lot.'

'What about your dad?'

'A right Jack-the-Lad by all accounts. He had the chat, the flash car with a personalised number plate — the lot, she was a naïve teenager and he was much older.'

'What happened to him?'

'Same old story — once she got pregnant, he didn't want to know.'

'I'm sorry.'

'Don't be, Peter, I'm not. Anyway if they'd got wed I'd have the same name as a film star.'

'Natasha Malone?'

'No stupid, that's me mum's name — Natasha Richardson. He was called Richardson, Tom Richardson.'

'Where is he now?'

'Don't know — he never came to see us. To be honest I think he was a bit dodgy. He's probably inside by now — or charming his way into someone else's knickers. Come on I'll take you to meet a friend of mine.'

They left the Japanese Garden and retraced their steps. Peter put the remains of their lunch in the bin by the main entrance and was about to cross the road heading towards the Station, when Natasha pulled him back.

'My friend's down here,' she pointed left down the road. They linked arms and walked down the hill, skirting the outside of the new park, until they reached the land that had been set aside for building. A billboard advertising the proposed new housing stood in front of the unrestored part of the old park, which was an overgrown wasteland enclosed by a shiny new wire fence, ten feet tall.

'It all used to be like this,' said Natasha said. 'It was a wilderness with burnt-out cars and druggies sleeping rough.'

She took his arm and they walked down towards the river and a strange modern building that Peter realised was a pub.

'This where you friend lives?'

'The Britannia? No—he doesn't drink.'

The pub was busy and the car park behind it almost full. She walked to the far end of the car park then climbed a steep bank into a wooded area at the rear with Peter in tow. There was a fence in the wooded area that she began to walk along, pushing between the fence and the trees.

'What are you looking for?' asked Peter.

'A way into the park. This is Liverpool- you put up a fence, someone will find a way in.'

'Why?'

'Why do you think? To see if there's anything worth nicking inside!'

Peter pushed through the undergrowth after her.

'I thought we were going to see your friend?'

Suddenly she appeared next to him, but on the other side of the fence.

'Told you so—they've cut a proper doorway with wire cutters the other side of that tree.'

By the time Peter was through the fence she was already some distance ahead and he had to run to catch up with her.

'We're trespassing!'

'Yes.'

'What if they've got dogs?'

'Dogs?—to guard what—weeds?'

There was a large red object surrounded by overgrowth on the far side of the field and, as they approached, Peter could see that it had been left over from the festival. It was a sculpture of a monster's head about three metres high.

Natasha tapped the sculpture.

'Meet my friend George,' she said.

'This monster?'

'He's not a monster, he's a dragon called George.'

She slipped through the overgrowth into the open mouth of the dragon and Peter followed. Inside was like a small cave and the tongue was a stainless-steel ramp that sloped up to an open doorway at the back of the head. Natasha sat at the bottom of the ramp and Peter sat next to her.

'Why George?' he asked.

'I was only little and my mum brought me down her. She told me all about the park and the fun she'd had as a kid. She put me on her shoulders so that I could look over the fence and then I saw him. He looked so fierce; I was scared. To calm me down my mum said that he was a good dragon who looked after a princess and protected her from the scallies. I wasn't scared of him then and every time we came here she used to have to bring me to see George.'

'But why George?'

'I misunderstood something my cousin had said about St George and the dragon; I thought it was about a saint and a dragon called George. I thought all dragons were called George.'

Peter tapped on the roof of the dragon's mouth, it was hollow.

'What was he?'

'A children's slide. You walked along his back and came in through the door at the back of his head and slid down his tongue. There was a competition on *Blue Peter* to design an attraction for the festival.'

'Have you been here since?'

'Lots of times. This was my secret place when I was growing up. If everything became too much at home or school I'd come here and talk to George. He was never angry and he'd always look after me — I was his princess wasn't I?'

Peter smiled and put his arm around her.

'I came here when I ran away from home,' she said. 'I was being bullied. Have you ever been bullied?'

'No — not really.'

'You're lucky; it eats away at you. I was only eleven, small with red hair and freckles — I was bound to be picked on. She was two years older, a fat cow called Charlene Bickerstaff. She and her cronies terrorised the younger kids, stealing their dinner money and sweets. If you tried to resist they'd rough you up and flush your head down the loo. They always seemed to pick on me, so much so that eventually even my friends kept out of my way.

It all got too much for me. One day — it was the week before the summer holidays — I decided to run away from home. I went off to school as normal then hid around the corner until I saw me mum leave for work. I crept back into the house, changed into my tracksuit and made myself a week's supply of jam butties and packed them into the haversack I'd had for girl-guide camp, together with a two-litre bottle of pop and my sleeping bag. I left Mum a note telling her not to worry and, as an afterthought, took a disposable barbeque and a dozen sausages.'

'And you came here?'

'Yes—I always felt safe here. I put my sleeping bag on the slide,' she patted the shiny metal, 'and used pieces of cardboard to block up the door at the back and to keep out the wind.'

'How long were you here?'

'Only for a night—the bizzies found me. I had some of the sausages for breakfast. Someone saw the smoke and thought some scallies had set fire to a car in the park and called the police. I was eating my third sausage and feeling pretty miserable and cold when a face leans in through George's mouth. I screamed and he laughed, then came to sit next to me.

"You Natasha Malone?" he asked.

I just nodded.

"Good," he said, "any chance of one of them bangers? I'm starvin'—been looking for you all night."

He radioed in to the Station to tell me mum that I was safe, then we shared the sausages and I told him about Charlene Bickerstaff. He told me his name was PC Wilson, Darren Wilson, and that he ran a youth club. He asked me to come along. Told me not to worry about Charlene, he'd been bullied as a kid until he decided he'd had enough. He'd seen the film 'Karate Kid' and decided to learn a martial art and now he taught it. He said the discipline and spiritual enlightenment would help me cope with whatever troubled me. It wasn't about violence it was about self-respect and inner contentment. A Zen philosophy to life.'

'So, what happened next?'

'I jacked in ballet—I was never going to be Darcy Bussell—and took up Taekwondo. Darren was right; the discipline and order helped build my confidence. I was very agile due to the ballet and the moves came easily. I spent the summer practicing and quickly got my first few belts, but by the end of the holiday I was beginning to get nervous. It's one thing to practice for an exam; it's completely different if there's a chance you'll have your head flushed down the loo if you fail. The police had had a word with the school, but I knew the bullying would start again once the dust had settled. It was only the end of the second week when Charlene and her cronies cornered me in the girl's toilets.'

'What did you do?'

'She went to flush my head down the loo so I broke three of her fingers and knocked out one of her front teeth.'

'Oh.'

'That's *Scouse Zen*, hit them first—worry about the philosophy later. She left me and me mates alone from then on. She works in Sayers in town now, selling cakes. She's still an ugly bitch though—like a docker in a frock, as me nan used to say.'

Natasha went quiet. Peter understood why.

'Sorry about your nan—it was so sudden.'

'I saw her the night before and she was right as rain. Still off her trolley mind you and talking as though her dead sister was coming to visit her—but she seemed well enough.'

'How's your mum taking it?'

'She phoned me from her hotel in Llandudno this morning. Her and Maggie sound like they're having a right laugh; it'll take her mind off things. Looks like we'll have the flat to ourselves for a few more days.'

Natasha lay back on the stainless-steel slide and stretched her arms.

'You know I feel a bit light-headed after that wine,' she said. 'Alone with a strange man, a girl could get taken advantage of.'

'I suppose she could, but I wouldn't do that would I?'

'Oh, I think you should.'

She pulled him towards her by his collar and kissed him.

Later they lay side by side staring up at the inside of the dragon's mouth.

'Shouldn't we share a cigarette? She asked.

'Why—neither of us smoke?'

'But they always do it in films and it's dead romantic.'

He propped himself up on one arm and stared down at her.

'Can I ask you something?'

'Yes I did.'

'Pardon?'

'I always do with you, Tiger.'

He blushed and she laughed.

'Watch the quiet ones,' she said: 'that's what me mum told me. Now I know what she meant.'

'No, I was being serious. Will you move in with me? The tenants are moving out of my old flat soon and the department are going to re-new my contract. I'll soon be able to stop working at the apartments. What do you think?'

'Yes.'

'That it? No umming and arrhing?'

She smiled and started to put on her shoes.

'Let's celebrate,' she said, '- last one to the Britannia buys the champagne.'

She leapt up and ran off towards the hole in the fence.

By the time he'd found his left shoe and put it on she had disappeared into the wooded area by the fence. He ran after her—then he heard a scream. He reached the fence and called for her but there was no reply. It was already starting to get dark and it was difficult to find the hole in the fence amongst the trees. He forced his way through the bushes calling her name, disorientated by the alcohol and panicking. Eventually his fingers touched the cut edge of the wire fence and he knelt down and pushed his way through.

'Stay on your knees. Don't do anything stupid!'

Directly in front of him was a man dressed in black. A large, black hat covered most of his face and as he was in the shadows Peter couldn't see his features. What he could see was the gun in his left hand.

'We've got your little friend—although she needed some persuasion to come with us.'

Peter looked around and called out 'Natasha' but there was no reply.

'If you want her back—and in one piece—you'll do what I tell you to do.' The man threw a package onto the ground in front of him. 'You give this to the tenants of 13C tomorrow morning at 9am—no earlier. Understand?'

Peter nodded. His mind tried desperately to catch up.

'You say a man in black handed it to you at the desk a few minutes before. Understand?'

Peter nodded again.

'Do like I've said then you'll get 'mighty mouse' back in one piece; if not—you'll get her back a piece at a time in a jiffy bag, first an ear or a finger, perhaps her nose next. I'll keep her alive while I do it.' The man laughed.

'Eventually you'll have all the parts and you can stick her back together if you like.'

'Why?' Peter stared open mouthed.

'Don't you worry about that. It's *family* business, no concern of yours. Just do what I tell you for both your sakes — OK?'

Peter nodded.

'Stay on your knees for five minutes or I'll make her pay. Remember — 9am and no earlier.'

The man slipped away into the darkness and Peter stared at the package in front of him. It was a small jiffy bag. A shiver went down his spine. It was addressed to: 'The Lone Ranger and Tonto — Apartment 13C.' Peter picked it up and shook it; he didn't know why — he did it automatically. It made no sound. The silence was broken by a car driving away at speed. Peter stayed on his knees. Any minute he expected Natasha to appear and explain it all. He waited and waited but she didn't return.

It was completely dark when he finally left the wood and walked back to St Michael's Station. Thirty minutes later he was sitting on the sofa in Michelle's flat and still in a daze. He tried to clear his head by pretending that Natasha would be home soon. He washed the dishes in the sink and did some ironing, then realised that he hadn't fed her parrot. He filled a dish with nuts and raisins and poured a tot of rum into one of its water bowls then took the cover off its cage. It woke up.

'Cap'n wantz eez grog!'

'I've got it here.'

Peter opened the cage and placed the food inside.

'Satisfied now?' he said.

The parrot ignored him and started to eat. Peter was about to leave the room when he heard tapping. He looked around but couldn't see what was making the noise; it seemed to be coming from the window but the flat was on the 10th floor so that seemed unlikely. He pulled back the curtains and was surprised to see a large herring gull on the window ledge. It looked at him with its cold yellow eye then tapped on the glass twice.

'Shoo!' Peter waved his arms but the gull looked unimpressed and tapped again. Peter didn't fancy opening the window to scare it away; he'd heard that they could be quite aggressive. There was a staring match. The gull's cold, yellow eye was unblinking and impassive. Peter blinked first swore and pulled the curtains closed.

After a short pause, the tapping recommenced. Peter sat on the sofa and stared at the parcel. He tried to make sense of the day's events but the parrot squawked and talked to itself as it continued eating and the tapping on the window continued. He found it was impossible to think clearly.

Suddenly the tapping stopped. Peter looked up. The gull must have flown off he thought. He was about to stand up and draw the curtains to check when the parrot squawked and fell off its perch. He rushed over. It was lying on the floor of the cage with its eyes open.

'Perfect- could it get any better? Now I've killed her parrot.'

The parrot blinked then coughed.

'For fuck's sake,' it said, 'that hurt.'

'What?' It had never said that before.

'You deaf as well as stupid kid?' The parrot climbed back on its perch and preened its feathers, 'Jesus- I think I've got mange.'

Peter stared. 'You can talk? — really talk — not just repeat things?'

'Course I can talk. Don't you remember our little chat last time? Don't you remember your old friend Frank?'

'Frank?'

'You're the one repeating things.'

'But you were a dream.'

'Let's cut to the chase. I haven't got time to talk about God again. That's why I'm here — we need you to do something for us.'

'Us?'

The parrot looked up to the ceiling. '*Us*' it whispered, and winked.

'No, no, no — you're a hallucination brought on by stress; you're not talking to me; it's just my mind playing tricks. I'll put the cover over your cage and go to bed and it'll all be OK in the morning.'

'He'll kill her you know. Even if you do what he says he'll still kill her — it's what they do.'

'Who?'

'Vampires.'

'*What?* No — you're mad. No — *I* must be mad because I'm talking to a parrot about vampires.'

'You've got to take the parcel to them tonight so they've got time to plan what to do.'

'If I do that he said he'd chop her up and kill her.'

'He'll do that anyway, kid. The only people who can stop him are the couple in 13C.'

Peter sat on the sofa and held his head in his hands. The parrot started eating the nuts.

'Sorry kid, I'm starving; been out and about all day; mouth's like the bottom of a parrot's cage.' It sniggered to itself, then took a sip of the water. 'Jesus! Is there booze in this?'

'Rum.'

'Perhaps being a parrot isn't so bad after all.'

'How did you get here? I thought you were a pigeon.'

'Look kid — let's get this straight, I was an angel *disguised* as a pigeon.'

'You're not a pigeon?'

'Give me strength. I was a pigeon — then I was a gull — now I'm a parrot.'

Peter leapt up and pulled the curtains open. The gull was still on the ledge but it was motionless.

'Left him on pause.'

'Who?'

'Neville — the gull, lovely guy but a bit dull.'

'Why aren't you a pigeon anymore?'

'Needed to cover more ground. It's not very fast by pigeon — that's why we borrowed Neville.'

'Borrowed?'

'Yeah borrowed. We won't harm him; he won't remember a thing.'

'So why are you a parrot now?'

'You wouldn't let me in and we need to talk.'

'Even if I believe you — why should the people in 13C believe me?'

'Because I'll tell you something that'll make them believe you.'

'What?'

'That the man in black is called Steve Kelly and he died here in 1862.'

'Why should they believe that?'

'Don't worry kid, they'll believe it. Just make sure you tell them everything that happened and get the parcel to them as soon as possible — it's her only chance.'

'But why Frank? Why me? Why Tash?'

'Can't say kid, but the management have a special interest in you two.'

'What?'

The parrot shrugged its wings, 'Don't suppose I could have some more rum kid? It's cold out tonight and I've still got work to do.'

Peter topped up the water dish with rum and the parrot drank all of it then climbed back on the top perch and suddenly froze. There was a loud screech from outside as the gull fell off the ledge and simultaneously the parrot fell off its perch.

Peter walked to the window and looked out. A lone gull glided past the window and winked.

He waved to it and whispered, 'Good luck Frank.'

Then he looked at the parcel in his hand and went to get his coat.

St Nicholas's

Kelly had already caught a small cod and thrown it back into Queens Dock. He didn't often eat what he caught these days because it was the fishing that was important not the catch. He was distracted; he should have been thinking about was what bait to use next, whether he should use lugworm again or to try a piece of squid, but, as his float bobbed on the choppy Mersey, all he could think about was what bait to use for Melville. He popped a chocolate in his mouth. He must be addicted to them, he thought, if he wasn't able to give them up, not even after what had happened to him. Deciding to use the squid, he baited his hook and checked over his shoulder before casting his line. His right hand still felt strange and he found the flick of the wrist rather clumsy as the baited hook curled out into the river. He sat on his chair and watched the float glinting in the sunlight. There was something about sitting on a river bank that always calmed him. It went back to his childhood when it had been the only place he had felt safe and in control. With sunlight shimmering on the water, he couldn't see the cranes of Cammel Laird's on the opposite bank and for a brief moment he was back beside the Mississippi of his childhood. He remembered those hard times so many lifetimes ago.

Kelly didn't know where he had been born or what name he had been given at his christening — or even if he'd been christened at all. All he remembered of his early life was hunger and dirt. He had no memory of a mother, just a drunk called 'Pa' who called him 'Kid' and found any excuse to beat him. Most days he fished. If he caught more than they needed to eat, he would sell it and hide the money under a loose floorboard in their shack. At night he'd cook fish for him and Pa and, if he hadn't caught anything, he'd get a thrashing for being lazy and often one for no reason at all. He'd lay on his straw mattress at night, count his coins and dream of running away. When he had enough to buy a little boat he would sail down the mighty Mississippi as far away from Pa as the river would take him.

One night he came back late. The fishing had been good and — careful to hold back enough of the catch to spare him a beating — he had sold the rest of it and tied the coins in a piece of rag in his pocket. The shack was deserted when he arrived and he set to work starting a fire to cook the fish. He was beginning to fillet the fish when the door flew open and Pa burst in, very drunk and in high spirits. That made him anxious; you never knew how Pa would behave when he was drunk. He'd either hug you or nearly beat you to death. He came and put his arm around him and made a rambling speech about a birthday present which made no sense. It made his flesh creep, but he was grateful that Pa was pleased and it seemed he would escape another beating.

Then he noticed that the loose floorboard had been moved.

He tore free from Pa's embrace, ripped up the floor board and scrabbled in the dirt beneath. It had all gone.

Every coin, all his dreams, his only chance of freedom. Pa leaned over him, grinning, not so jovial now, holding his belt in his hand and cursing. Pa drew back his hand the buckle of his belt glinting in the candle light. He couldn't remember exactly what happened next: just the flickering candlelight and the silence afterwards, punctuated by the cracking of the fire. He remembered that he wiped the blood off the filleting knife, set fire to the shack and slipped away into the night. At dawn he hid in the railway sidings and boarded a freight train going west. He had no way of knowing it but it was his birthday; he was eight years old.

Something tugged at the line and Kelly snapped back to the present. Then the line went slack and his prey escaped. It was time to call it a day. He packed away his fishing gear and, throwing the remaining bait in the Mersey for the gulls, walked back to his apartment. As he passed the disused Dock he remembered Pearson, so prim and proper, all starched collar and gold pince-nez. He'd expected him to be a coward and easy to break but he'd been surprisingly tough. It had taken a lot of persuasion to get Melville's name out of him, let alone anything else. Then that oaf, Jack had hit him too hard and killed him. And that would have been it if he hadn't found the half a silver dollar in Pearson's waistcoat pocket and guessed its significance. Without that coin they'd never have lured Melville into their ambush. However whether that was a good thing or not Kelly still hadn't decided. That was the strange thing about being a vampire: should you hate the person who made you into one or embrace them as a blood brother or sister? After all Melville might have wanted to kill him in the first place even if the end result was immortality and almost unlimited amounts of fun for over a century and a half. In fact, Kelly couldn't bring himself to be grateful; he didn't understand why but no one ever was. Take the Malone girl, she certainly wasn't grateful was she? Kelly reached up and touched the missing tip of his right ear and pondered suitable retribution. He walked around the outside of Albert Dock and up onto the Strand, by that route he avoided passing the statue of Billy Fury because he no longer found it amusing. Its appearance seemed to be mock him.

Kelly was soon back at Rumford Court. He packed away his fishing gear and changed his clothes. He decided to return to St Nicholas's Church where it had all begun, to see if that would help focus his thoughts. He walked the short distance and sat on a bench by the Church entrance trying to remember how the Churchyard had looked on the fateful night. The stone steps at the far end still went down to the Strand and the stone archway where he had first caught a sight of Melville was still there, but all the grave stones had been removed and in their place was an ornamental garden with benches. Kelly now understood that although he hadn't been able to see Melville well in the darkness, Melville would have been able to see them clearly with his superior night vision of a vampire, something that Kelly had had ample opportunity to exploit on his own nocturnal hunting expeditions for 'soft centres'. Why hadn't Melville killed him properly like Jack and Annie? That was a puzzle. He'd thought long and hard about it over the years and had decided that Melville might accidently have got some of his own blood or saliva on the blade, leaving the scene before his victim, Kelly, was completely dead It was a simple error and everyone did it once or twice—but you always lived to regret it. He rubbed his missing piece of ear and thought of his own carelessness.

He searched in his left hand pocket and took out another chocolate. Kelly still didn't understand: why had the box of chocolates exploded at Cat's flat? — that part still confused him. No one had been expecting him and it wasn't until he told her that she knew he'd been responsible for her son's death. People didn't usually have explosive boxes of chocolates sitting around in case of emergencies, did they? Some people were so strange it made you wonder about human nature. At least, he killed people because he needed to. Well, almost: sometimes he did it for fun but that wasn't the point. He was a vampire; he was supposed to do it. If there was a job description for being a vampire 'merciless killer' would be top of the list, well before 'good with animals' or 'has a sweet tooth and a charming personality'. He sat and chewed the chocolate and tried to work out what had happened.

He had just opened the box, he remembered, when Sheryl's phone rang in his pocket. He was sure it would be Melville so he threw the box of chocolates to one side and pulled the phone out of his pocket with his right hand — and then the box exploded. He came round to find the room on fire and blood was obscuring his vision. When he tried to wipe the blood from his eyes he discovered that his right hand had taken most of the force of the explosion. He used the belt from Cat's coat to make a tourniquet and used the back stairs to leave the block before the fire brigade arrived. He'd managed to get to his car and, after the fire engine, police and ambulance had arrived, drove with difficulty back to Rumford Court. Luckily the 4x4 was automatic and the tourniquet worked well, enough that he managed to get back safely without passing out with pain or loss of blood. The next few days were still a bit of a blur because he'd spent them passing in and out of consciousness until his wounds began to heal and the pain began to ease. After a week he'd felt well enough to go out. He'd bandaged his wounds and, with dark glasses and a scarf to disguise his face, he'd bought food and newspapers in a supermarket in Old Hall Street. The newspapers informed him that the police were still investigating the explosion and had linked it to one on the Wirral that had killed a retired war hero. Kelly had felt relieved because there was no mention of them looking for anyone of his description but remained confused as to the reason for the explosion. He'd also been interested to read that an unnamed woman had been found at the scene having fallen or jumped from the building prior to the explosion, and that she was presently in a coma in the 'Royal'. Perhaps they'd get to have that encore one day after all. The following day he'd boarded a flight for the States to recuperate. Revenge would have to wait.

He'd stayed away until he was completely healed. His right hand still hurt and he would have expected that sensation to have gone by now but other than that he felt fine. He'd only been back in the city for a few days and he'd done very little other than fish in the Mersey and try to work out if all the things that had happened since the attempt on his life on the pier were connected. Were they all part of someone's master plan or just coincidental? Kelly was old enough and wise enough to know that he shouldn't do anything rash until he understood his opposition. He already had some facts to go on.

To begin with, someone who called himself Geoff Davies had tried to shoot him on the pier. He thought he recognised the man from somewhere but he couldn't remember where or when. Also, the man obviously didn't know he was a vampire otherwise he'd have known that a bullet to the head wouldn't kill him. And that meant that he must be unconnected to Melville or Sheryl Malone.

Then someone, Davies or someone else, had killed Richardson, Doyle and the boys but not made any attempt to take over the clubs, drugs or prostitution. Why had they done it? So that they could get to his safety-deposit box and take his things? So that could be Melville? But if he'd known about him then surely Malone would have known who he was and why he was after Melville? Finally someone had tried to blow him up with a booby-trapped box of his favourite chocolates.

No matter how hard Kelly thought, he couldn't see any single connection between all these events. So the best course of action was probably to treat each problem independently and hope that, as he sorted out each one, he would finally be able to make sense of it all.

He'd already tried to trace Geoff Davies but without success and, since he'd killed Cat, he couldn't find out anything about the bomb from her, so that only left Melville and Malone. Kelly knew that Malone had survived the fall and it was reasonable to assume that she probably thought that the explosion and subsequent fire had killed him. His best course of action was to keep his head down and keep a close watch on them until the time was right but it was hard to be inactive when the memory of what they'd put him through was so fresh in his memory. He stretched out on the bench popped another chocolate in his mouth and looked around the Churchyard. There was now a plinth with a ship's bell where his body had lain after Melville had stabbed him that faithful night.

Kelly remembered laying on the cold gravestone feeling his life slip away then hearing a scream which sounded far away and a torch shining in his eyes, then a police whistle and a delirious ride in a Hansom cab to the Infirmary. He remembered little else of that night. They had expected him to die and had called a priest who administered the last rights, but to every one's surprise he made a miraculous recovery. A week later he was sitting in his rented rooms in Bixteth Street examining Pearson's watch, which he'd recovered together with his pistol from the pawn brokers.

Lizzie, the young whore who attended to all his needs, had brought him a note from William O'Neil that had been pushed through the letter box. That night he had waited as agreed in the Churchyard of St Nicholas's with a bag of sovereigns and a bottle of whisky to keep out the cold. Most people would have felt uncomfortable to be somewhere where they had so recently nearly died but somehow Kelly felt safe. He sheltered under the Church porch, sipped his whisky and waited for his man. O'Neil was the contact at the US Consulate who'd told him about Pearson and his agent. He was an ex-local detective who worked for the Federal spy master, Thomas Dudley. O'Neil had no allegiance to either side in this war and was happy to provide information for money and Kelly was waiting to make his final payment.

O'Neil had arrived late and drunk and began arguing about the money, claiming that he'd no idea that Pearson would be killed and demanding more money for the addition risk he was now taking. Dudley had cross questioned everyone and a major investigation was now underway. Pearson and his agent, Melville, had both disappeared without trace but somehow the plans for the *Oreto* had been left at the Consulate. Unfortunately the ship had sailed before the British government could impound it. They wanted a scape goat and O'Neil had no intention of being it. Kelly tried to calm him down and offered some whisky from his bottle. O'Neil knocked the bottle to the ground, breaking it and spilling its contents. Kelly picked up the broken bottle and waved it at O'Neil telling him to calm down. What did he have to complain about? He hadn't been stabbed and was being well paid for his troubles. O'Neil lashed out again and this time he hit Kelly in his chest close to the knife wound. Kelly grimaced in pain and then everything went into slow motion. Kelly had been seized by a rage unlike anything he'd experienced before. He took the broken bottle and thrust it into O'Neil's neck, twisting it again and again. Next thing he was looking down at the writhing man as he bled to death and that was when he was suddenly overcome by a strange, unnatural urge to taste the blood. He dropped the whisky bottle, knelt down leaned over — and lapped at the fresh blood as it poured from O'Neil's neck. O'Neil tried half-heartedly to push him away but Kelly was too strong for him and, as O'Neil's strength ebbed away, he became silently resigned to his fate. Satiated, Kelly walked back to his rooms, his mind a turmoil of conflicting emotions; he was simultaneously repulsed and aroused by his actions.

The *CSS Florida/Oreto* had left Liverpool a week previously and in some haste in order to avoid being impounded by the British government. On the same day, a ship had left Hartlepool carrying supplies and armaments for the *Florida* with the intention of transferring them in the Bahamas. It had been decided overnight that Kelly was now a liability and, to avoid any embarrassing police investigations, he needed to disappear forthwith. The following morning he was aboard a fast mail clipper bound for the Bahamas and a rendezvous with the *Florida*.

He travelled under an assumed name and with false documents but something else had changed about him. He didn't understand what it was and, as he stood on deck and watched Liverpool recede into the mist, he was unable to make sense of his emotions. Why had he drunk O'Neil's blood? It had seemed so natural and now he felt energised. Perhaps he was losing his mind? The ships bell rang indicating midday. He took Pearson's watch from his waistcoat and set it to ship's time. He read the dedication — from Pearson's fiancée, Sarah-Jane to her beloved James — then closed the watch and returned to his cabin.

That had been over a century and a half ago but as he remembered the theft of that precious watch from his safety-deposit box it brought him back to the present. He stood up, needing to walk off his frustrations, and left the Churchyard by the steep stone steps at the far end and walked down the Strand towards Melville's apartment block. He knew he was taking a risk but he was sure that Melville would assume he had died in the fire and, dressed as he was, he didn't think he would be recognisable from a distance. As he approached the block a group of angels spilled out of the supermarket near James Street Station, at first he was confused then realised that it was a hen party. They were all dressed identically with pink wings and halos and were obviously quite drunk. Kelly smiled as he passed by he'd never had an angel before; perhaps he might be able to collect one on his way back. He passed Melville's apartment but kept his head down and walked straight into a stag party dressed as convicts. They were wearing brown overalls with black arrows on them and carrying plastic ball and chains. They were laughing a joking and clustered around him but Kelly's mood had changed he pushed through them and shook them off but he couldn't shake off his own memories.

§

It was 1846, young Kelly been riding the trains and his luck for about a year when he was caught by the railroad detectives and sent to the local orphanage. Within the week he tried to run away. They quickly caught him and, after a whipping, locked him in the cellar with bread and water for two days. A week later he tried again but this time, in the struggle to apprehend him, he cut a train guard with a homemade knife. The orphanage sent him to a reform school.

The stated aim of the reform school was to reform young offenders by a combination of religious instruction and hard work. They would be taught a trade and the three R's and instructed in the Bible, but the teaching was rudimentary, sufficient to add up a bill or write a shopping list and little else while the religious instruction was more 'fire and brimstone' than 'love thy neighbour'. Order was maintained by fear and corporal punishment.

He was nine years old with curly blonde hair and freckles, and he had a name: Stephen Kelly. The orphanage had called him *Kelly* because they had an old shirt with that name from a previous pupil and it saved them making a new name tag. The *Stephen* came from one of the railway guards who'd caught him. He'd run headlong into a thorn bush trying to evade capture and got pricked from head to toe by thorns — just like St Stephen and his arrows the guard had joked.

The school was divided into two dormitories, each one under the control of a guard. All the inmates were expected to be trained in one of the three basic trades: blacksmith, cobbler or carpenter. Sundays were devoted to religious instruction and Church services and focussed on the inmates' need to repent for their past sins in order to achieve redemption. There was little chance of escape in the short term so Kelly decided to bide his time and learn what he could that might be useful in the future — and to enjoy the regular food.

Unfortunately the guard of his dormitory, a man called Witney, had little interest in moral redemption and much interest in young boys. Kelly, young and cute, was quickly receiving one-to-one instruction in certain of the seven deadly sins. Whitney began by showing him affection and giving him small gifts — and the first time he gave Kelly a candy bar, Kelly had no idea what it was or even how to unwrap it. Whitney plied him with candy and 'little Stevie' revelled in the attention. Whitney told him stories about his time at sea and showed him how to tie knots. Bit by bit the affection became abuse but, because Kelly had nothing to compare it to, it seemed to him to be natural and loving. Whitney never forced him to do anything and it was only with hindsight that Kelly could see that he was a predatory paedophile; at the time he saw him almost as a surrogate parent. Kelly tried hard at his studies in order to please Whitney. He found that reading came easily and within a year he could read and write well. All thoughts of running away were gone; for once in his short life he felt happy.

One afternoon Stevie came back from the cobbler's classes with his first set of boots to show Whitney but Whitney wasn't there; another guard was in his room. The school was assembled that evening and the principal gave a lecture about the sins of the flesh and moral deviancy. Guard Whitney had been arrested on a charge of gross indecency and would not be returning to the school. The police were unsure whether they had sufficient evidence to press charges but the governors of the school had decided to dismiss him forthwith. Stevie ran back to his dormitory in tears looking for Whitney, but Whitney never returned.

It seemed that the authorities felt that Stevie was somehow responsible for Whitney's moral decline, and the following week he was transferred to the other dormitory and the blacksmith's classes. The guard of this dormitory was a lazy drunk who reminded him of Pa and order was maintained by an older boy, a bully called Jackson. Jackson was a stocky muscular thug, three or four years older than Stevie. He ran the blacksmith's class and was mainly interested in casual sadism and young boys. Whitney had been manipulative but gently; Jackson was violent and cruel and gained most sexual satisfaction from the humiliation and submission of his victims. The first day in blacksmith's class Stevie was set to work pumping the bellows for the furnace. He had to kneel close to the coals and pump hard to get the fire to draw. Jackson and his cronies stood around jeering.

'Too hot for you boy?' Jackson laughed. 'Let's cool you down.' They clustered around and spat on him. 'Cool enough now, Tadpole?'

Suddenly two of them grabbed him by the arms and pulled him away from the bellows. They dragged him over to the anvil and held his right arm firmly on its top surface. He could hear Jackson raking the coals then he appeared with the hooked rake. He waved in in Stevie's face and jeered: 'Gotta mark wats yers boys. So no one steal it.' He pressed the hot iron against Stevie's flesh and chuckled: 'Yer mine now Tadpole.'

Jackson was true to his word and Stevie learned what it was to be owned. Another year passed of cruelty and abuse but, however sadistic or humiliating it was, Stevie never cried; he just waited and made a pledge to himself that he would never be owned again. In future he would be the owner, the one in control, he would have his freedom. Every night he lay awake and dreamed of fishing on the Mississippi and waited for his moment to come. Only Jackson stood in his way.

Almost a year passed before Stevie had his chance of revenge. The blacksmith's class was housed in an old barn and the furnace was in one corner with room beside it to allow carts to be brought in for repair. A large block and tackle hung from the ceiling in the centre to allow the cart wheels to be lifted off and on. When not in use this was pulled to one side and secured to the side wall with a chain. Stevie worked out that, if the chain was released, the block would swing down and hit someone standing in front of the furnace. All he had to do was arrange for that someone to be Jackson.

The following morning he slipped out of the canteen while everyone else was still eating breakfast. He had a short length of rope in his pocket that he used to tie the block to the side wall. He passed one end of the rope out through a knot hole in the wall of the barn then looped the chain loosely around the block on the inside so that it appeared to be securing it to the wall. In fact, all the weight of the block and tackle was held in check by the rope. He'd used a special knot that Whitney had taught him that was used on ships, a knot that could support heavy loads but be easily released by a gentle tug on one end of the rope.

Jackson arrived and shouted at Stevie to start stoking the furnace and pumping the bellows to begin another day. Stevie did as he was told and soon the coals were burning red-hot. Stevie took a pair of metal tongs and pushed them into the coals. He knew that although they looked cold and black they would soon be too hot to handle. He carried on pumping the bellows and waited for the guard to arrive. Time ticked by and Stevie watched the tongs. All was in place and he knew what he had to do but he was worried that someone would notice them and spoil his plan.

Eventually the guard arrived and as Stevie greeted him with a cheery, 'Good morning Officer Graham,' he seemly absentmindedly reached out and took hold of the tongs. Stevie screamed and dropped the tongs. The guard looked at the burn and told him to put in under running water and, when he returned a few minutes later with a large blister in the palm of his hand, sent him to the sick bay. Jackson cursed him and found another boy to pump the bellows.

Half an hour later, Stevie was back; the orderly had bandaged his hand because the doctor hadn't arrived yet. The guard was outside the barn smoking, right next to the knot hole with the rope hanging through it. When Stevie looked in through the open door he saw Jackson standing over the other boy shouting at him with his back to the door and his hands on his hips. Unfortunately, the guard looked at his bandaged hand and told him to report to the office for light duties and, as Stevie turned to walk away, he realised that his chance of revenge had nearly gone; he had to do something and he had to do it now. He turned back as though about to ask for further instructions then pretended to trip over and, as he fell forward, put out his good hand as if he was trying to save himself. While falling in a heap at the guard's feet, he grabbed the rope and tugged. The rope snatched back and disappeared through the hole. Officer Graham bent down and picked him up and teased him about being so clumsy—then they heard the screams from inside the barn.

They ran inside. The block had hit Jackson, stunned him and knocked him into the hot coals. The young boy had managed to pull him onto the floor and stood over him screaming. Jackson was screaming too. He was writhing on the floor, his hands and face horribly burnt. Large blisters were forming over his flesh. The guard shouted at the young boy to get the doctor and pulled the Jackson onto a work bench. The smell of burnt flesh hung heavy in the room, reminding Stevie of roast pork. So Jackson really was a pig after all he thought, and smiled to himself.

The doctor arrived, shaking slightly and smelling of alcohol. He examined the screaming Jackson, shook his head and went outside to talk to the guard in private. Stevie was now alone with Jackson who had stopped screaming and was whimpering softly.

Stevie bent close to Jackson's blistered face. 'Too hot for you boy?' he whispered then spat in Jackson's face.

It took Jackson ten days to die; within six months Stevie was branding his own tadpoles.

§

Kelly wondered why he'd thought about Jackson after all this time. He'd been so deep in thought that he'd absentmindedly walked through the shopping mall and was now at the Church Street end of Paradise Street amongst the hotdog and burger vans. The van he was standing in front of sold 'Hog Roast'. He smiled to himself and joined the queue.

A few minutes later he was sitting in Chavasse Park finishing his meal and looking up at Melville's apartment block. He'd worked out which set of windows were Melville's and had noted over the last few days that the blinds were being opened and closed which meant that Melville was still there. All he had to do was work out how to get into Melville's building. The exterior doors were controlled by key-fob sensors and the main door manned by the concierges with CCTV. Obviously, he could wait until he came outside but the timing would be difficult. Last time he'd got in with the aid of luck and that stupid concierge but he wouldn't be so lucky next time. He didn't want this opportunity for revenge to slip away again; he'd nearly caught up with Melville a hundred years ago but Melville had slipped through his fingers. If he let him get away again it could be another hundred years before their paths crossed again. Kelly decided that he needed another pair of hands now that Doyle and the boys were dead. He'd need to call in a few favours and get some new thugs and weapons. He threw the remains of his 'Jackson' burger in a waste bin and walked into town to call on an old adversary, Joe Chan

Kelly called ahead and arranged for a meeting in an hour's time in China Town. He was walking along Renshaw Street when he saw a shop selling antiques and curios and went inside to kill some time; he didn't want to arrive too early. The shop was dark and filled with a mixture of antiques, collectables and to Kelly's eyes rubbish. He smiled to himself as he went from glass case to glass case; things he had once thrown away were now somehow revered and collectable: faded postcards, mismatched china, — the detritus of the last two hundred years, polished and catalogued and with a hefty price tag. Then he spotted an interesting fossil at the back of one of the cabinets and called the assistant to get it out for him. A rather bored-looking young man opened the case.

'Ammonite, 250 million years old.' The young man read the tag. 'You collect fossils?'

'I had one once but it got away — I'll take it.'

At the till, Kelly was about to pay when a display of cut-throat razors reminded him of the last time he'd nearly caught up with Melville, back in 1918. The razors were open displaying their blades and Kelly read the makers' names. Some makes he had once owned but some were new to him. He laughed.

'I'll take that razor too,' he pointed at the display, '- third from the right.'

'This one — the 'Kelly's Matchless'?'

Kelly held it in his hand. The blade was slightly rusty and there was a small chip out of its cutting edge; it was still sharp although you couldn't shave with it. He held it up to reflect the light. The blade was etched, 'Kelly's Matchless' and stamped 'made by Robert Kelly and Sons Liverpool'.

'Perfect,' he said.

'Be careful,' said the assistant, '- it's sharp. You don't want to cut yourself.'

'Don't worry, I've no intention of cutting *myself*.'

The assistant put the fossil into a carrier bag and Kelly slipped the razor into the side of his ankle boot. He'd always carried one this way in the past; people rarely check your shoes if they search you. There was no harm in having a little security of his own he thought. He checked his watch and walked slowly up Renshaw Street, down Nelson Street and through the Chinese arch into Chinatown. Tourists were posing in front of the arch and taking photographs but, because it was late afternoon, most of the restaurants were empty. He stood outside one of the largest and took a deep breath. He wasn't frightened — there was little that frightened him since he was usually the one doing the frightening and he knew all the tricks — but he was unsure how this meeting would go. He needed weapons and man power to deal with Melville. Time was short, and it was better to make a deal with an old rival than risk losing Melville and his possessions again.

He pushed open the heavy restaurant door and entered the dark interior. A large Chinese man by the side of the door silently indicated that Kelly should turn around and raise his hands. The man searched him casually, neglecting to check his boots.

'Sloppy', thought Kelly.

The man looked in the carrier bag and pulled out the fossil.

'What's with the fuckin' rock?'

'It's a fossil — 250 million years old.' Kelly smiled his crocodile smile.

'Couldn't you afford somethin' new?' The man laughed.

Kelly debated whether to hurt him now or later, decided later, took the fossil from him and put it back in the bag. At the back of the restaurant another man sat eating alone. He assumed that this was Joe Chan. They had never met face to face; they knew one another only by reputation. Kelly walked slowly down the restaurant and stood in front of the eating man in silence. Kelly knew all the tricks: try to make him do the talking, keep him on edge and keep him guessing. He'd used them all many times himself. He stayed silent. The man was large and overweight but muscular. He was oriental with a shaved head and was wearing a white, silk shirt with the sleeves rolled back and a large napkin tucked into his collar. An expensive suit jacket was hung on the back of his chair. He studiously ignored Kelly and continued to eat. The minutes ticked by in silence. Kelly felt more comfortable; they were obviously still wary of him. Whoever broke the silence would lose the initiative. The man finished his meal and pushed his plate to one side. He looked up and Kelly was surprised by two things, the bright blue eyes and the Scouse accent.

'Mister Kelly — thought yer wer' dead.'

'Perhaps I still am, Mr Chan.' Kelly took the seat opposite without invitation.

'What d'yer want then — buryin'?'

'The loan of two of your boys will do.'

'Why shud I give yer anythin'?'

'Because I'll give you my supply chain and a list of my clients. I'm leaving for the States soon and don't plan on coming back—once I've dealt with a little problem.

'Hey Mike, yer lazy git, get Mr Kelly a drink,' Chan shouted across the room.

A bottle of sake and two glasses promptly arrived and Chan poured two large measures.

He raised his glass and toasted Kelly: 'May you live a long life.'

Kelly smiled, 'I intend to.'

The next few hours Chan plied Kelly with drink and Kelly pretended to get drunker and drunker while he wondered what Chan was planning. The alcohol had little effect on Kelly and he pretended not to notice that Chan was topping up his own glass with water. Kelly decided to bide his time and see where it was going and if he could use his talents to gain some advantage. Chan obviously had no intention of giving him what he wanted.

Eventually Chan decided the Kelly was ready and suggested that they give him a ride home and they could discuss business another day. They helped him out through the rear entrance while he pretended to have problems walking. A large Mercedes was parked in the alley behind. Kelly climbed happily inside, making sure to take his carrier bag with him, and began to sing. They drove to the old disused docks to the north of the city, Chan sitting in the rear with Kelly and the doorman driving. The mood was friendly until they were safely parked behind a rotting warehouse.

'We home?' Kelly giggled and then feigned confusion, 'where are we?'

Chan pulled a gun from his jacket.

'Time for yer buryin',' he said and prodded Kelly in the ribs. The driver opened the door then remained with the car watching out for any possible witnesses while Kelly walked unsteadily ahead of Chan.

'But ... I thoug'- we had a deal?' Kelly slurred his speech and stumbled while gradually twisting the carrier bag with the fossil inside around his right hand. The razor was in his left boot.

'Yer a dead man already; I'm just tidyin' things up.'

Once they were around the edge of the warehouse and out of view of the driver, Kelly pretended to trip and, as he did so, he slipped his hand into his boot and pulled out the razor. Chan came up close behind him and was about to prod him with his foot when Kelly spun around and, using the carrier bag as a sling shot, hit Chan full in the face with the fossil. There was a satisfying crunch of bone and Chan fell back unconscious. Kelly unfolded the razor, cut Chan's throat and drank his blood — with relish.

The driver sat waiting in the car with the engine running; they'd done this several times before and he knew that his boss would soon return alone. When Kelly stumbled around the corner of the warehouse carrying his carrier bag and zigzagged uncertainly towards the car, the driver assumed that Chan had changed his mind and perhaps they'd done a deal after all. Kelly wove drunkenly towards the car and then knocked on the driver's window. The driver opened it.

'Where's Mr Chan?' he asked.

'Here.' Kelly tipped the contents of his bag through the window and on to the driver's lap. Chan's head stared up at the driver who only had time to scream once before a bullet blew off the side of his face.

Kelly put Chan's gun in his pocket and searched the car thoroughly. He found an Uzi sub-machine-gun and a bag containing a Taser and some cartridges. In the car boot there was a bag full of individually wrapped sachets of cocaine and some heroin. Kelly had no interest in these but he did have a use for the bag. The drugs would give a motive for the murders if he left them behind.

He scattered some of the drugs on the quay side and, having a change of heart, put a few sachets in his pocket. He dumped Chan's body and his head in the car boot, released the handbrake and pushed it down the slipway and into the dock. The Mercedes floated on the surface for a little while then gradually slipped beneath the surface. Kelly stood on the edge of the quay with his bag of guns and waved to the dead driver as the water lapped over him.

'Thanks for the lift,' he murmured.

It took him twenty minutes to walk back to Rumford Court where he left the guns, then he walked back into the city. He now had the weapons but not his extra pairs of hands. There was no time to be too choosey he needed to find someone soon; it was important to act before Melville realised that he was still alive.

Early that evening Kelly was sitting once again in Chavasse Park watching the windows of Melville's apartment thirteen floors above him. He took the razor out of his boot and licked the blade clean. He loved the taste of fresh blood. Then he looked at the blade where it read: 'Kelly's Matchless — made in Liverpool' and smiled to himself. They had much in common him and his razor because he was *made* in Liverpool too, made into a vampire by Melville and Melville would soon be made to pay for that. In fact he'd paid for it once already even though he didn't realise it yet. Kelly ran his finger along the razor's edge, savouring its sharpness.

§

December 1917, Kelly was on board ship and had just left Queenstown in Southern Ireland bound for New York and was feeling pleased with himself. He'd been gun running for the IRA for a few years but, since the failure of the Easter Uprising the previous year, he'd been on the run. He was travelling under a false identity and when the ship left British waters he could at last breathe a sigh of relief. Of course, if the British realised where he was they would telegraph ahead and have the ship intercepted but that was very unlikely to happen.

He sat in the smoking room with a large bourbon and had just lit himself a celebratory cigar when the waiter offered him the British newspapers from the day before, both national and local newspapers. The ship had sailed from Liverpool and the local papers were from Liverpool. He was flicked through the papers and puffing happily on his cigar then froze: There was a small article in the *Liverpool Daily Post* about the awarding of the VC to an officer in the King's Liverpool Regiment. There was a small black and white photograph of the man and beneath it, his name — Melville.

So Melville was in Liverpool but Kelly was on a ship heading across the Atlantic. The only thing he could do was sail to New York and then sail back again as soon as he could arrange passage. He had to hope that the authorities in Liverpool wouldn't recognise him from his Irish police warrant.

It was three weeks before he was back in Liverpool and it took him another week to confirm that Melville had already left. Rumour had it that he'd fallen out Charlotte Truscott, the wife of one of his dead comrades who blamed him for her husband's death. Perhaps she'd know where he'd gone?

He broke into Charlotte's house. He was easily able to overpower her and tried to get her to talk without leaving any marks but she knew nothing of any use. He had some fun with her but, when he grew bored, he filled a bath with hot water, gagged her and tied her hands and feet with bandages so as not to leave any marks. Then he held her in the bath and slashed her wrists with her husband's razor and waited as she bleed to death in the warm water. It was a waste of blood but he needed the death to look like suicide. Once she was dead he untied her and left her floating in the bath of blood and, to add to the illusion of a suicide, he took one of her letters and soaked it in the spilt bath water thereby making it illegible and apparently a suicide note. He'd hoped that her death would bring Melville back for her funeral and he waited and waited but Melville never reappeared. He tried to trace Melville over the next few years but to no avail, and now a hundred years had gone by before this second chance had come his way. He needed to plan carefully so as not to waste it.

§

Kelly was about to leave and head home when he saw a young couple walking through the park towards him. She was young and small with red hair and wore a nurse's uniform and the young man was taller and slightly scruffy. Kelly recognised the man. He waited until they'd passed then followed. They walked down the steps onto the Strand and kissed. The young man went in through the main door and the girl continued along the Strand towards James Street Station. Kelly followed.

He now had Chan's weapons but still needed a spare pair of hands and some way to get into the apartment block at will. When he'd first recognised Melville all those weeks ago he managed to get in by tricking the young concierge. He was unlikely to be so lucky next time. What he needed was some leverage to guarantee the concierge's cooperation and also his silence—perhaps the girl would give him that. He was following close behind her and not watching the road when a van nearly hit him as it turned into the resident's car park entrance. The driver sounded his horn and pulled up next to a metal bollard. He wound down the window, swore at Kelly then pressed a button on the bollard. There was a buzz and a voice answered.

'Hello.'

'Delivery for Grimes 14C.'

'OK—pull into the loading bay on the left.'

The metal car park door opened automatically and the van drove inside. Perhaps entry would be easier than he'd imagined. He could still see the girl some distance further up the Strand and, decided it would be wise to have an alternative plan as well. Kelly hurried to keep her in sight. He caught up with her at the entrance to James Street Station and followed her onto a Merseyrail train.

Thirty minutes later he was outside a nursing home on the Northern outskirts of the city. She'd been inside for several minutes and he was considering leaving when he saw her coming down in the glass-walled lift from the first floor pushing a wheelchair. He watched from behind a large tree as she pushed the wheelchair and its female occupant into the nursing home garden. Now he could get a closer look at her; she was small and young with freckles and bright red hair. Perfect, if he was careful he could blackmail the concierge to get to Melville and Malone and still get to keep the girl for himself. Then he recognised the woman in the wheelchair and laughed out loud — it was Sheryl sister. This couldn't get any better. The girl turned and looked in his direction but couldn't see him in the shadows and, after a few minutes in the garden, they went back inside. He waited in the shadows for an hour until the girl emerged then followed her home.

She crossed over the rail line on a metal footbridge into a scruffy council estate where a collection of tower blocks huddled around a semi-derelict shopping centre. Most of the shop units were boarded up, their steel shutters sprayed with graffiti. The only shops open were a kebab shop and a twenty-four-hour off-license. The girl was a little way ahead of him and she seemed anxious. She was making sure that she kept out of the shadows and continually looked around her. Eventually, and with obvious relief, she entered one of the tower blocks. Kelly rushed after and entered the door close behind but the she'd gone, although the lift was silent which meant that she'd taken the stairs. Perhaps her flat was on the first floor. He now knew where to find her when he needed her even if he didn't yet know the flat number nor her name.

He walked back to the station deep in thought. He had the weapons and an address but still no extra pairs of hands to help him so one problem was not yet resolved. Then, as he approached the footbridge, his path was blocked by two youths. They were young, late teens or early twenties. One was taller than the other, but other than that they were almost identical. Close-cropped hair, tracksuit bottoms tucked into white socks and trainers, black hoodies and earrings — the unofficial uniform of a local scally. Kelly knew their sort because he'd been something similar himself many years ago, even if the clothes and the accent had been different. He attempted to push past but the taller lad blocked his way.

'Sorry Pal — this is a toll bridge,' said the taller youth and they both laughed.

'Pay up or else,' said the shorter one.

'Or else what?'

'Or else I cut yer fuckin' throat,' said the shorter youth, brandishing a flick-knife.

'Dear me,' said Kelly, 'is that the best you can do? Not very frightening is it?'

'Shut the fuck up and give us yer money!'

'Cut 'im — show the fucker yer mean business,' said the taller youth.

Kelly moved quickly. He took hold of the knife hand of the shorter youth with his left hand and twisted; the lad screamed and dropped the knife. At the same moment

Kelly hit the taller one in his solar plexus with his right elbow with all his force. The taller youth collapsed to the ground winded and Kelly picked up the flick-knife and held it to the shorter youth's throat.

'What's your name?' he asked, pressing the knife hard against the flesh.

'L- Lewis.'

'Who's this?' Kelly nodded towards the taller youth who was doubled up on the floor.

'Me brother, — Dean.'

Kelly let go of Lewis, folded up the flick-knife and handed it back.

'Would you boys like a job?' he asked.

He was walking back to the station with a spring in his step. It had been a successful day: he'd killed two people, hired two people, found a new victim and acquired weapons. Anyone else would be satisfied but the night was still young. He touched the fossil in his pocket and turned away from the station. Kelly walked back towards the nursing home and Sheryl's sister.

The following morning he picked up Dean and Lewis in his 4X4 and drove through the Mersey Tunnel to an old industrial unit in Birkenhead on the opposite side of the river. The squat brick building was next to a dry dock and the huge warship being dismantled there cast a permanent shadow over it. The noise from the dock made conversation impossible and Dean and Lewis exchanged nervous glances. They didn't trust Kelly and were worried that he'd brought them here to take his revenge on them for trying to mug him the previous night. Lewis fiddled with the flick-knife in his hoodie pocket.

Kelly unlocked the steel shuttered door of the industrial unit and held the button at the side of it down while a motor rolled the door open, then he drove inside and once they'd all got out of the 4X4 he closed the door behind them. The unit had probably once been a small engineering works. The floor was painted with yellow lines denoting walkways, and large expanses of bare concrete marked where machinery had once stood. What light there was came from large, overhead skylights set into the high ceiling. It was surprisingly quiet inside.

'Good sound insulation.' Kelly smiled his crocodile smile. 'No one can eavesdrop on what I get up to.'

Dean and Lewis exchanged a worried look.

'Mr K? — Lewis an' me wer juz wundering wh-?'

'I'm not paying you to think. Just to do what I tell you — understand? You're hired muscle — scum.'

They glowered at him and Lewis gripped the flick-knife in his pocket tightly.

'I was scum once,' Kelly smiled. 'I understand what scum wants. Provided you boys do what I tell you to do, I'll see you get what you deserve — OK?'

'OK — long as yer not takin' the piss.'

'Excellent! Come over here; I've got something for you both.'

They followed him to a large work bench that ran the full-length of one wall. He took a black bag from under it and emptied its contents onto the steel surface with a clatter. He turned around with a gun in his hand and pointed it at the brothers.

'Glock 19,' he said.

They put up their hands

'What the fu- ' Dean looked at Kelly then at Lewis.

'Safety catch is here on the trigger.' Kelly pointed to it. 'Catch,' he said and threw it to Dean.

Dean looked at the gun and then at Lewis. Kelly picked up another gun.

'Uzi sub-machine-gun,' he said. 'Safety here — rapid fire here.' He threw it to Lewis who nearly dropped the heavy weapon.

'What the fuck?' said Lewis, 'We in a fuckin' war or summit?'

'Sort of,' said Kelly, '- just a little one between old friends. You two are my foot soldiers and I'm your general. Remember, in a war, if you don't do what they tell you to do — you get shot. Understand?'

Dean clicked off the Glock's safety catch.

'What if I shot you instead?' he asked.

'You'd make me very angry,' Kelly wasn't smiling now, 'You really don't want to get me angry. It would only end in tears — your tears.'

Dean held Kelly's stare but something about the eyes chilled him and he looked down.

'Only jokin' — no offence like.' Dean lowered the gun and clicked on the safety catch.

'Good. I'll make sure you get what you deserve — OK?'

'Thanks — Mr K.' both replied and smiled at one another. Kelly smiled too. The two brothers seemed quite excited and began play-acting with the guns. He watched them with contempt; it was difficult to get good scum these days.

'OK, boys quieten down, we need to talk. I've got a job for you.'

Lewis held up his hand and Kelly paused.

'What?'

'Sorry, Mr K — I need a piss.'

Kelly waved a hand towards the office. 'The john's in there — be quick.'

The toilets were at the back next to the office. There were three urinals, two sinks and a cubicle, all in a decrepit state but still functioning. On his way out of the toilets, without washing his hands, Lewis spotted another door. Being curious and finding it unlocked, he pushed it open — it appeared to have been a communal shower-room. The back wall and floor was tiled and there were two shower heads. It all looked quite normal but then he spotted handcuffs attached to one of the shower heads and a long rubber hose on the floor. A pool of water had collected next to the drain in the floor, which was discoloured and on the wall there was a blood stain that hadn't been washed off. Lewis had found Kelly's torture chamber.

Two days later they were in a hired van outside of the industrial unit. In the back was an empty cardboard box. Kelly was running through the plan one last time.

'Remember -you wait until he's left the apartment. Then you drive up to the intercom and say — what?' Kelly was frustrated; they'd already been through this twice.

'Parcel for Melville 13 C?' said Dean slightly unsure.

'Good! Then?'

'We take the box to the flat, knock and when she opens the door, zap!'

'Good — next?'

'We cuff her and bring her back here.'

'Good. And what if someone gets in the way?'

Dean pulled out the Glock. Wave this at 'em and if they don't fuck off — shoot 'em.'

'Try not to shoot anyone unless it's absolutely necessary. Do you understand?'

'Yes Mr K.' they both nodded.

'Don't underestimate her. She's stronger than you think. Don't take any chances — OK?'

They nodded and drove off. Kelly shook his head and went back inside the building to wait.

They drove through the Mersey Tunnel and parked on Albert Dock. Dean walked up to the gates which opened onto the Strand and watched the main entrance of the apartment block opposite. He had a photograph of the man and woman to help him identify them. Kelly had told him that the man went for a walk every morning and that he'd be gone for about an hour. Once Dean saw the man leave he and Lewis were to go and get the girl as quickly as possible. Eventually, a tall, dark-haired man came out of the main entrance and walked off along the Strand. Dean checked the photo carefully then went back to the van and drove out of Albert Dock, along the Strand, around the island opposite St Nicholas's Church and back down the road to arrive at the entrance to the apartment car park. He pushed the intercom button.

'Delivery for Melville 13C.'

The intercom crackled then a voice said: 'OK — pull into the loading bay and use the service lift on the left.'

They parked the van and, smirking, opened the boot and carried the empty cardboard box to the lift. They'd found it in a skip, it had originally contained a 50" Plasma TV and they fooled around pretending it was very heavy.

Dean took out the Glock and clicked the safety catch on and off.

'Show time ar' kid.'

Lewis laughed and pulled out the yellow Tazer.

'Zap! Zap! Zap! Like fuckin' Star Wars.'

'Ready?'

'Ready.'

Dean pressed the lift button.

'Don't screw up Lew; I wouldn't want to piss off that bastard Kelly.'

'No way—you didn't see that fuckin' torture chamber of 'is. I wouldn't wanna be this tart wer 'ere for. Poor cow—God knows what she or 'ere fella 'av done but 'es really got the 'ump.'

'Who does 'e think 'e is anyhouse Lew? Fuckin' Zorro? All in black, that big 'at—'e even wears them gloves all the time. 'e's a fuckin' weirdo if yer ask me?'

There was a 'ping' and the lift arrived. They high-fived one another.

'Game on Dean.' Lewis threw the empty box into the lift and Dean pressed the button for the 13th floor.

Twenty minutes later, they were parked in Albert Dock once more but their mood had changed.

'What the fuck 'appened there?'

'Fuck me—I 'aven't a clue Lew. Who was the other bastard? Kelly didn't warn us about 'im.'

'No 'e didn't Dean—an' that midget. She was like Bruce fuckin' Lee. I thought she woz gonna break me fuckin' neck. Wot ar' we gonna do? You lost 'is gun. Kelly'll fuckin' kill us.'

'Wot about you Lew? You lost 'is Taser.'

'Let's fuck off in the van an' never come back.'

'He'll find us and e'd be even more pissed off. We've still got the Uzi; if we wait 'til they come out we cud get lucky.'

'OK- but if we don't, an' 'e asks yer'd like a shower, run for yer fuckin' life.'

Next day they were sitting in Kelly's 4X4 in a small side street close to Abercromby Square watching a small Peugeot.

'OK,' said Kelly trying to remain calm. 'It's simple—don't screw up this time.'

Dean and Lewis were in the front seats with Kelly behind them.

'No worries, Mr K. We won't—will we Lew?'

'Because of your incompetence Melville and Malone are now on their guard. We now need another way to get to them. You follow this car and the driver; you keep me informed of when and where he goes. It might take a few days, but sooner or later we'll get him and the girl alone. When that happens you tell me—do you understand?'

They both nodded.

'If he leaves the car, one of you follows him and calls me—I'll tell you what to do next—the other waits with the car. Understood?'

They nodded.

'Get this right and you'll get what you deserve; screw up and you'll wish you were never born—understood?'

'Course, Mr K. Yer can bank on us—can't 'e Lew?'

'Deffo.'

'OK—he'll be here for a few more hours. Take me back to Rumford Court, then come straight back.'

ALBERT DOCK

It had been a busy few weeks for Lathom since he'd found the access codes to the 'Oreto Holdings' account in Kelly's wall-safe. Once back home a few minutes on-line was all that was needed to transfer all the money to his Swiss bank account. He was now financially secure and need never work again. Initially he'd intended to carry on as before, undertaking the odd contract just to keep his hand in, while using the additional capital to acquire something special for his collection. However, the more he thought about it, the less he wanted to take any more risks. The last few 'jobs' hadn't gone as smoothly as he would have expected and he was concerned that small errors were creeping into his work. Lathom realised that, if he carried on, the combination of increasing age and alcohol consumption would eventually prove fatal to him.

A week after Richardson's murder, Doyle's car had been recovered from the River Severn, and, as Lathom had hoped, the resulting police investigation linked both incidents. According to an article in the *Shropshire Star*, the dead men had been identified as criminals from the Merseyside area and forensic evidence linked them to the murder of a businessman in Liverpool. It was assumed that their murders were either as revenge for that murder or were related to drug dealing.

Lathom now knew that he was safe and could carry on as before but he had somehow lost his enthusiasm for removing scum. Perhaps it had to do with Richardson's murder; the death of a friend always made him feel vulnerable. Surprisingly that still seemed to apply even though he was directly responsible for it. Unfortunately, since Doyle's visit to his cottage, it no longer felt like the sanctuary it once had been. He was increasingly relying on alcohol to get to sleep and the faces of dead friends and enemies plagued his dreams. Money being no longer an obstacle, he decided to make a clean break, to move to Liverpool and concentrate on writing his book on the 'King's' regiment. Within the week he had arranged for another antique dealer to take on the lease of his shop and had begun, surreptitiously, to sell his collections.

A week later he stood outside a new apartment block in the city centre waiting for the estate agent to arrive. A harassed-looking young man in an expensive suit approached him with a bundle of papers under one arm and his right hand out stretched.

'Mr Laidlow? I'm Hugh Foster from Greenley Residential.'

'Lathom.'

'Sorry, Mr. Lathom? It wasn't a very good line, thought you said Laidlow. Shall we go on up?'

They walked past the reception desk to the lifts. There was a man behind the desk tapping at a keyboard.

'Twenty four hour concierge and CCTV,' said Foster.

Once inside the two-bedroom, 13th-floor apartment,

Foster gave a well-rehearsed sales pitch. Lathom ignored him and stared out of the large lounge window at Albert Dock.

'This is our last apartment with a river view,' said Foster. 'It was one of the show apartments and all the furniture is included in the sale. I'm surprised it hasn't sold at the reduced price; perhaps it's because it's on the 13th floor? — You're not superstitious are you?'

'I'll take it.'

'Pardon?'

'Do you take cash?'

A week or so later the move was almost complete. Since the apartment was fully furnished, Lathom left all his own furniture in his cottage. He hadn't decided whether to sell the cottage or let it out. The move would be a fresh start; he'd sold most of his collection through the trade without raising any suspicion and had only brought his clothes, books and a few items of sentimental value to the new apartment.

He waited for a lift with the last two boxes. It arrived with a 'ping' and he struggled inside it, dumped the boxes on the floor was about to press the button for the 13th floor when he found that the button was already illuminated. The other occupants of the lift were a tall man with dark hair and a small, red-headed woman.

'Hey Lee, things are looking up. We've got a pirate moving in,' said the woman.

'Sorry?' said Lathom.

She pointed to the handle of a cutlass sticking out of the top of one of the boxes.

'Is your parrot and eye-patch in the other one?'

Lathom laughed. 'Sorry to disappoint you; I'm an antique dealer.' he held out his hand. 'Bob, Bob Lathom.'

'I'm Sheryl and this is Lee.'

There was a 'ping' and the lift door opened. Lathom made his excuses and went to pick up his boxes.

'Lee, don't just stand there; give Captain Bobby a hand.'

The tall man picked up a box and they both followed Lathom to his door.

'Thanks — this is me, 13F.'

'That's handy; we're 13C.' The woman pointed to the door on the opposite side of the corridor. 'When you've fed your parrot and run up the 'jolly roger' why don't you pop in for a drink?'

Lathom tried to find an excuse but somehow got talked into it which he immediately regretted — he preferred to remain anonymous. He unpacked his boxes, put the books on his bookshelves and his few personal items on his dressing table. He sat on the sofa and stared at the cutlass. He still didn't know why he'd kept it; he should have disposed of it because it linked him to the car in the river, but he felt attached to it because it had saved his life. The remaining items were the Webley and one of his 'Chow Mein' specials. 'Better safe than sorry,' he thought. Twenty minutes later he knocked, reluctantly, on the door of 13C, clutching a bottle of wine.

'Hey Lee! Its Captain Bobby, come on in luv.'

'It's Bob actually.'

'Lovely — red wine.' She took the bottle from him. 'That's dead kind, Bobby — my favourite; I'm a sucker for anything red.'

She took a small penknife from her tracksuit pocket, cut off the foil with the blade and used its corkscrew to pull the cork.

'That's handy,' said Lathom.

'You never know when you'll need a sharp knife, Bobby. Always best to be prepared.'

Lathom wasn't one for socialising but the evening flew by. As the drink flowed the conversation became less stilted and it seemed only natural to order in some pizzas from the Italian restaurant on Chavasse Park. He and Lee discovered a shared passion in military history. In fact Lee became quite animated, even more so when the conversation turned to whiskies. Lathom loved his Scotch although Lee preferred Irish.

The following morning, nursing yet another hangover and regretting the 'blind tasting challenge' which had ended the evening, Lathom left his porridge half-finished, picked up his note pad and left his apartment. On his way to the lift he knocked at 13C to hand over a book that he had promised to Lee the previous evening.

'Hiya Bobby.'

He was taken aback. Sheryl had her hair cropped in a crew-cut and bleached peroxide blonde. She laughed at his confusion.

'Just a red wig, Bobby. Had a mad moment a few weeks ago and shaved my head for charity.' She giggled.

'What charity?'

'Bootle donkey sanctuary.'

'Pardon?'

'Lee hates it, thinks I look like a leprechaun, cheeky bugger.'

'Said I'd drop this off for Lee.' Lathom handed her the book.

'He's gone for one of his walks. Want to come in for a coffee?'

'I'm off to do some research at the library.'

'No worries, Bobby. Pop in any time.'

'It's Bob actually, not Bobby.'

'Sorry, luv. You remind me of me Uncle Bobby; he was a good lad too.'

Lathom left the apartment through the main entrance and was about to head towards the Central Library to continue his research as he had planned. However being called Bobby after all these years had brought back difficult memories. Other than his parents the only other person who had called him Bobby was Billy Flanagan. Lathom changed his mind; the research would have to wait. He crossed the Strand into Albert Dock. He needed to see where Billy had been murdered one final time.

It was a restaurant now, the tourist ate their meals unaware of the old warehouse's gruesome past. Lathom sat at a corner table and stared at the large, cast-iron hook in the ceiling above. It now supported an ornate light fitting; the last time he'd been here, Flanagan's body had been hanging from it.

He raised his coffee, and muttered the toast: 'Absent friends.'

Lathom needed something to shake off his melancholy; he left by the rear door onto the Dock itself. An old tug was moored on the opposite side. The upper decks were covered in plastic sheeting and a large sign on the dock side gave a brief history of the ship and appealed for funds and volunteers to enable its restoration. He decided to look round it.

The *Daniel Adamson* was built in Cammel Laird's shipyard in 1903 as a tug/tender. She was intended to work as a tug and also to carry passengers across the

Mersey and, having survived a hard life on the river, she was now in the process of being restored by a preservation society. Lathom was given a guided tour of the ship by one of the volunteers. Lots of work remained to be done. There was friendly camaraderie amongst the enthusiasts that reminded him of his early days at the Bridewell, when the humour of the local bizzies made the job seem like a game. That was before Billy's death, after that nothing had ever been the same again

An hour later, he had become a volunteer, joined the preservation society, bought some merchandise and agreed to return that following day to begin work. On his way back to the apartment he visited the Maritime Museum to check on something he'd researched. On the top floor there was an exhibition of shipping on the Mersey; models of various sizes charted the evolution of the port and of ship-building in the area over the centuries. In one corner there was a small display to mark the 150th anniversary of the American Civil War, chronicling Liverpool's role in the conflict. There was a small, wooden model of a sailing ship, the *CSS Florida* (*also known as the Oreto*), built by William C. Miller and Sons at Queens Dock 1862. Lathom smiled. He'd searched on-line to find an explanation of the Oreto Holdings accounts name and this was all he'd been able to find: a Confederate warship built in Liverpool, the subject of the painting in Kelly's flat and a similar age to the gun and watch he'd found in Kelly's the safety-deposit box. Was it in some way connected to the photo album he'd also found there? Perhaps one of Kelly's ancestors had some link to the ship?

Lathom spent the afternoon in the Central Library doing some research for his book on the 'King's' Regiment, and while there he took the opportunity to borrow a book on Liverpool's role in the American Civil War. That evening he was trying to work on his book but he found himself preoccupied with memories from the past. He'd spent too many years trying to blot them out, but now he was back in Liverpool again they hung over him like a black cloud. He decided that the only way to deal with his past was to confront it face to face. He picked up his wallet and checked its contents then pulled on his coat.

It was only a short walk down the Strand to the 'Baltic Fleet'. Many of the surrounding houses and warehouses had been cleared for redevelopment and it now stood alone, a strange triangular-shaped pub on the busy dual carriageway. It seemed to glow from a distance as though dropped from the above into the middle of a building site. As he drew closer. He felt that he was looking at a window into his past. Through the large bay window he could see customers clustered around the bar and he half expected to see familiar faces sitting at the table in the window. He was transported back to an evening forty years before.

§

Lathom opened the door and pushed his way through the drinkers and thick clouds of cigarette smoke to a large, round table in the bay window. A man at the table looked up from his pint.

'Wer 'ave you been Bob?' asked John the custody sergeant.

'Just doing some paperwork,' Lathom replied.

'It's your round.'

During the week they used drink in 'Rigby's' near the Bridewell, but Fridays were special; provided they weren't on the rota to work they always started the weekend in the 'Baltic'. Lathom pushed his way back to the bar and squeezed into a space at the far end next to a tall blonde man. The man smiled and made space for him and Lathom took a note from his wallet and tried to attract the barmaid's attention. While he waited, he lit a cigarette and watched the barmaid. She was young and pretty and he tried chatting her up every Friday — and was always politely brushed off. It was common knowledge that she was 'going steady' with a bloke from Manchester.

'Plenty more fish in the sea,' the lads reminded him.

'Hiya Bob. What can I get yer, luv?' she asked.

'Usual Jean. One Guinness, two bitters, a mild and a packet of salt-and-vinegar crisps.'

'What yer doin' tonight?' she asked as she poured the drinks.

'Nothing special. Few pints and a curry later — why?'

'I'm knockin' off early tonight if yer interested.'

'What about ... erm?'

'Davey? Given 'm the elbow.'

'What time do you finish?'

'Nine'

He picked up the tray of drinks and winked at her. 'See you later.'

When he turned with his tray of drinks he noticed that the blonde man had gone but left his drink behind untouched.

It was nearly nine o'clock, he hadn't mentioned his date with Jean to the lads because he knew they'd only 'take the mickey' and, when they decided to move on to another pub, he made up an excuse to stay. He was leaning on the bar nursing his final pint and sharing a secret smile with Jean, when Billy Flanagan rushed in.

'Hi Bobby. Where are the boys?' he asked.

'Gone up town, not sure where — why?'

'Got a tip-off about our man. Thought I could do with some back-up — what you up to?'

Lathom smiled and nodded at the barmaid, 'Got a date with Jean.'

'You're a dark horse, Bobby.'

'Can it wait until tomorrow?'

'I'll be fine — see you tomorrow.' Flanagan winked. 'Don't do anything I wouldn't do.'

Lathom watched through the window as Billy got into his car. The following day they found his mutilated body hung on a hook in Albert Dock.

§

Lathom sat on a bar stool sipping his beer. The table in the bay window was full of young revellers laughing and flirting. He thought back to that first evening with Jean. They'd left the pub and walked into the city centre, where they had a drink in the 'Vines' near the Adelphi. After that, they had gone to a club off Bold Street and ended up in his flat in Toxteth. Their relationship had only lasted a few months and the dark shadow of Flanagan's murder had always lurked in the background. No one had ever openly blamed him for Flanagan death, but he always felt that his colleagues thought that he was partially responsible. He had tried to cover up his feeling of guilt by throwing himself into the hunt for Flanagan's killer.

The game of cat and mouse with the IRA became deadly serious and the desire for revenge outweighed everything else. Suspects were taken to the Bridewell and a blind eye turned to the means of their interrogation while others had a short ride in Lathom's Cortina followed by a summary beating. Pubs and clubs owned by suspected republican sympathisers were raided, and substantial amounts of money were offered for any lead, but no information was forthcoming. The source of Flanagan's tip-off and the identity of the blonde man were never discovered. Flanagan's murder remained an unsolved case.

However irreparable damage had been done to the camaraderie of the team. Many felt unhappy with the methods used during the investigation and the Friday night drinks became a thing of the past. It had also damaged Lathom who had joined the force to help people, and who began to see no difference between the police and the thugs whom he had wanted to protect people from. He began drinking heavily to blot out his feelings and his relationship with Jean deteriorated rapidly. One day he came home from work, late and drunk, to find a note on the kitchen table and her flat key. A few months later he heard from a friend of hers that she'd gone back to her old boyfriend.

He sipped his pint and wondered what had become of her. He remembered the early days when all was love and laughter before dark recrimination and anger took their place. She was probably a grandmother now with hordes of grandchildren; she'd always loved children. What was he? He knew only too well — a lonely alcoholic, sitting on a stolen fortune and reminiscing about a wasted life. He ordered an Irish whiskey in memory of Flanagan, downed it in one then left the pub and walked away from the past and its oasis of light, back to his apartment.

The following morning was sunny and Lathom was in better spirits. He bought himself some overalls and steel toe-capped boots for working on the tug and, retrieving his bobble-hat from the boot of his car, walked over to the dock. He spent the morning trying to dismantle the circulating pumps for the steam engine with a volunteer called Owen. They hit it off immediately. Owen was ex-army and shared Lathom's black sense of humour. At lunchtime he bought a very expensive and disappointing sandwich from a café on the dock and ate it in the small galley on board with the other volunteers. By afternoon he knew everyone's name and felt very much one of the crew and it was agreed he would return in the morning to help Owen with the pumps — and he decided to bring a packed lunch.

He walked back to the apartment with a spring in his step. Perhaps retirement wouldn't be too boring after all; it was amazing what a difference a hard day's work made to his mood. He was sweaty and covered in oil and grease, and he felt ten years younger. He was about to cross the Strand at the pedestrian crossing when a large 4X4 jumped the lights. He stepped back just in time and as the car speed away he got a good look at the man in the rear. He thought he recognised him but dismissed the idea; he really would need to cut down on the whisky if he was going to start hallucinating about the dead. He made a quick detour to the supermarket on Hanover Street for something for tomorrow's packed lunch, then back to his apartment for a shower and an early night.

After his shower, Lathom sat down to write some more of his book then noticed the Civil War book that he'd borrowed from the library the previous day. He sat on his sofa and looked up *Oreto* in the index. There was a small chapter on the Florida/*Oreto* affair with several black and white photographs of the people involved: the financial backer, Charles Prioleau, the Confederate agent, Bulloch, and a couple of the officers and men on board the ship itself. He rummaged through his belongings until he found his magnifying glass and studied the group photographs carefully. It was fascinating. He cross-checked against the album from the safety-deposit box until he was certain: the tall, fair-haired man in military uniform was in both photographs. Then he looked in the index, and found 'Lieutenant Stephen Patrick Kelly' and a note in the chapter explaining that he was a member of the crew on the maiden voyage. So that was the link to Kelly and he could now assume that Lieutenant Kelly was probably one of Kelly's ancestors and that the watch and gun had belonged to this Lieutenant Kelly. In fact the more he looked at the photograph, the more obvious the link; Lieutenant Kelly and Steve Kelly were almost identical to one another, and the same cold eyes that had weighed him up on the pier stared out at him from the old photograph. In fact, the more he stared at the image the more it began to remind him of another face glimpsed briefly forty years before — but he dismissed that idea as a fantasy, shut the album and put it back on his bookshelf.

Once again Lathom was plagued by memories of the past and found that he couldn't get a particular image out of his head. All thoughts of an early night were forgotten and he reached for the bottle of whisky and, sitting on his sofa looked out of his window at Albert Dock — and remembered the first time he'd visited it.

§

Lathom could still remember the morning after that first date with Jean as though it were yesterday. He'd been making a pot of tea in his small kitchenette intending to take Jean breakfast in bed. He was feeling pleased with himself and thinking that things couldn't get any better when the call came from the local 'bizzies'.

By the time he parked his Cortina on the waste ground by Albert Dock there were already five police cars and two unmarked cars there ahead of him. He waved his warrant card at a nervous young constable and walked through the police cordon. The huge dock was black and derelict, surrounded by high security-fences and signs that threatened trespassers with prosecution and guard dogs. The dock gates had rotted away many years before and the once-vibrant dock was now filled not with water but with mud. Its windows were boarded up, the doors chained shut and small shrubs grew out of its silent quayside. He walked towards a group of officers standing outside one of the warehouses.

'Hi, Jim.' Lathom lit a cigarette and offered the packet.

'Hiya, Bob — fucking bad business this.'

'Yeah — who found him?'

'Night-watchman doing his rounds found one of the padlocks forced on the gate and called the local lads. They had a quick look around but they couldn't find anything; it was dark and the place is enormous. They thought it was just kids. Well there's nothing left to nick is there? They had the lead off the roof years ago.

'Why are they guarding it then?'

'Who knows? They say they're going to blow it up and use the rubble to fill in the dock and turn it into a car park.'

'Pity.'

'There's only one problem — no one in Liverpool can afford a fucking car.'

They both laughed then John took a drag on his cigarette and continued: 'Didn't find him until they did their rounds in daylight, then all Hell broke loose.'

'Can you take me to him?'

They walked around the side of the building into the inner dock. A uniformed policeman stood in front of a large warehouse-door facing the dock itself. They waved their warrant cards and he stepped aside to let them through. Lathom was aware the smell of vomit; there was a small pile of it by the door.

'First person who found him left that,' said John, '- don't blame him though — do you?'

Lathom looked up and took a deep breath. 'No, no -I don't.'

The body hung upside down from a hook in the ceiling. It was naked and its feet had been tied together. The hands were handcuffed behind its back and its head hung a few feet off the floor. The throat had been cut and the blood had drained into a large, white enamel bowl directly beneath its head. On the floor next to the body were a small, chipped enamel mug containing blood which appeared to have been drunk from and the victim's heart, which had been removed from the corpse.

It would have been impossible to identify the victim immediately because of the thick coating of clotted blood that obscured its features if the killer had not left a clue.

Pinned to the heart was Flanagan's warrant card.

§

Lathom was hung over again and he'd overslept but he'd promised to work on the tug today. He pulled on his greasy overalls and steel toe-capped boots and, grabbing his oily bobble-hat, took the lift to the ground floor. Phil the concierge was discussing the previous evening's football match with one of the security men and didn't look up, and the neighbour, Sheryl, was sorting through her mail. She looked at his clothes: 'going dancin'?'

Lathom was in a bad mood. He scowled.

'Bear with a sore head are we? You should take more water with it, Bobby.'

'What are you two up to today?' asked Lathom, recovering himself.

'Lee's gone for one of his walks; God knows where he goes pop in if you fancy a coffee.'

'Must dash; I'm late already.'

'Did you enjoy the film?' she asked.

'Thanks — I'll drop it in later.' He was trying to avoid answering the question.

He crossed the Strand and returned to Albert Dock

where he spent the morning working on the tug. When lunchtime arrived he realised that he'd left his sandwiches behind and decided to go home for his lunch.

Michelle was away for a few more days prior to the funeral and her daughter Natasha had offered to do the cleaning but as Sheryl had never met her she decided to do it herself. She was just finishing hoovering the bedroom when she heard the intercom buzz,

'We've got a delivery for Mr Melville. Shall I send them up?'

'Yeah—that's fine.' What had Lee been buying? He hadn't mentioned anything; perhaps it was a surprise for her. She put away the hoover. There was a knock at the door and through the spy hole she saw two men in overalls. She opened the door.

'Delivery for Melville,' said the taller of the two men.

They stood either side of a large, cardboard box.

'Come in.' She walked into the lounge and they followed carrying the box, closing the door behind them. She was about to tell them where to leave it, when they dropped the box and the shorter man produced a strange-looking yellow gun.

'What—?'

There was a flash of light and she felt as though she'd been hit by a bolt of lightning; she doubled over and fell to the ground. They stood over her. She was partially conscious but her limbs felt weak.

'Look at the size of 'er. Why did he want us to use the Taser?'

'Who cares? You fuckin' ask 'im. Give me an 'and to get them cuffs on 'er before she comes round.'

They pulled her hands together in front of her and she heard the 'click' of the handcuffs.

'See why Kelly wants 'er, she's a bit of alright,' said the shorter man. 'Fancy a piece of 'er meself.'

'Shut it Lew — 'e's a fuckin' nutter. Do what yer fuckin' told and keep shtum.'

Sheryl watched through half-closed eyes. The shorter man put a new cartridge in the Taser then they pulled her into a sitting position and slapped her face.

'Wakey, wakey sleeping beauty!' they both laughed, 'time to go *walkies*.'

She pretended to be groggy but her mind was working overtime. Who was Kelly? Why did he want her and for what? They obviously didn't know anything about her or her talents. There were only two of them and they would have to take her down in the lift. She smiled to herself; they wouldn't be able to use the Taser in a metal box. She'd wait until they got in the lift — then kill them. Just then, there was loud knocking at the front door of the apartment. The men told her to keep quiet, but it carried on. Then she remembered what she'd said to Bobby; it would be him.

'It's my neighbour, he said he'd come over; he knows I'm here.'

'Get rid of 'im,' said the taller man waving a gun in front of her face, 'or I will.'

They pulled her to her feet and, after removing the handcuffs, pushed her to the door. The taller man stood to the side hidden behind the door, the gun in his hand. The other man stood in the lounge doorway with the Taser at the ready. She didn't like the idea of getting Lathom involved but she needed some way to warn Lee in case she couldn't get away from them. The taller man opened the door, and prodded her in the ribs with the gun.

Lathom had finished his lunch and was about to return to the tug when he'd spotted the DVD on the coffee table. He enjoyed action films but preferred fact to fiction and somehow the idea of vampires in modern New York was too far-fetched for him. He decided to drop it off on his way out because he knew Sheryl would be home. He knocked on her apartment door but there was no answer and he was about the leave when the door opened slightly.

'Oh, Hello Mister Lathom how can I help you?' Sheryl asked.

At first he thought she was playing another joke and was about to say something facetious, then he noticed that she looked worried and decided to play along.

'Hello, Miss Malone. I wanted to return the film you kindly lent me. Would you like me to get you anything from the supermarket?'

Lathom was sure he could hear someone whispering to her behind the door but couldn't make out what they were saying.

'That's very kind of you, but I'm going out soon,' she replied, then silently mouthed, '*call Lee.*'

She took the DVD from him and the door slammed shut in his face.

Lathom stood in the hallway with a deep sense of unease. Something was definitely wrong. He went back to his apartment, called Lee and explained what had happened. As he hung up, he heard the door opposite close and instinct told him that he needed to act now.

He opened his own door and was just in time to see Sheryl and two men getting into the lift. She had her coat draped over her shoulders and they seemed to be escorting her. Lathom rushed after them and jumped into the lift just before the door closed. Sheryl stood with her back to the wall and the two men stood in front of her. The taller of them reached over and pressed a button on the keypad opening the door then placed a hand on Lathom's shoulder and pushed.

'Get the next one pal. This one's full.'

Lathom looked at Sheryl and she winked. This would need careful timing.

'There's plenty of room,' said Lathom. The man reached into his coat pulled out a gun and pointed it at Lathom. He smiled at his friend who laughed.

'I think you'll find it's a Glock,' said Lathom.

'Wha -?'

Lathom moved quickly. He grabbed the barrel of the gun with his left hand and kicked the man hard in the kneecap with his steel toe-capped boot. As the man toppled forward he head-butted him hard in the face and wrenched the gun from his hand.

Sheryl knew Lathom was going to do something, she'd seen him smile at her as he entered the lift but she was worried that he might get hurt. When she saw him make a grab for the gun, she jumped up and flung her handcuffed arms over the neck of the man in front of her, clasping her hands behind his head, then she choked him with the handcuffs. Bracing herself with her feet against the back wall of the lift, she kicked hard flinging him head first against the opposite wall. He crumpled and collapsed onto the floor and she was about to snap his neck when she looked up and saw Lathom with the gun and staring down at her.

'Next time I'll rip your head clean off,' she whispered.

The two men were sprawled coughing and spluttering on the floor of the lift.

'Keys!' said Lathom waving the gun at them. He unlocked Sheryl's handcuffs and then he searched them, suddenly a 'ping' announced the lift's arrival. The doors opened and the men ran off.

'Next time you get my stiletto up yer arse!' shouted Sheryl. She smiled at Lathom and pressed the button for the 13th floor.

'Nice one, Bobby. Where'd you learn that?'

'Special Branch—you?'

'Miss Williams' gymnastics class. Fancy a coffee and a chat?'

'Do you think they'll come back?'

'Bound to, Bobby. Scallies like them are too thick to take a hint.'

'Good.'

Back in her apartment, Lathom put the Taser, gun and handcuffs on the coffee table and Sheryl called Lee and told him not to worry, then she filled the kettle.

'Tea or coffee?'

'Whisky?'

She handed him a mug of coffee, and he took a sip then smiled.

'I put in a shot of Lee's special Irish whiskey. Don't let on—he'll only moan about it.'

A key turned in the lock and Melville entered. He was out of breath.

'What happened?' he asked.

'Two knob heads tried to kidnap me, but I got rescued by a knight-in-shining-armour.'

'Who?'

'Bobby.'

'What?'

'Bobby was in the police.'

'Special Branch,' Lathom muttered into his coffee.

'OK,' said Melville, 'start at the beginning and tell me everything.'

'Two scallies knocked at the door and when I answered one of them shot me with that thing.'

'Then what?'

'They handcuffed me and were taking me down in the lift when Bobby stepped in.'

'They say why?'

'Just that 'Kelly' wanted me.'

'Who's Kelly?'

'Don't know—I thought you would.'

'My 'dead man' was called Kelly,' Lathom interrupted.

Sheryl and Melville looked at each other and then at Lathom.

'How did you know he was a dead man?' asked Melville.

'Because I killed him.'

'What did he look like?'

'Tall, perhaps six one or two, slim and blonde.'

'Did he look like Billy Fury?' asked Sheryl.

'Who?'

'Get your coats; I'll show you.'

A few minutes later they stood in front of the Billy Fury statue in Albert Dock. It was late afternoon and the setting sun picked out the features of the bronze face.

'Is this your 'dead man', Bobby?' asked Sheryl.

'Yes.'

'I never knew his name,' whispered Melville. 'Now I understand what this is all about.'

They walked slowly back to the apartment, Sheryl and Melville arm in arm, talking and Lathom, feeling slightly uncomfortable, ahead. Just as they were about to leave the dock and cross the Strand, a white van pulled alongside them. The passenger leaned out of the window and pointed a machine-gun at Lathom.

'What's *this* then, you fat bastard?' said the man.

Melville reacted instantaneously. Running forward he pushed Lathom to the ground and threw himself on top of him. There was a 'rat-tat-tat', then the sound of the van accelerating away.

'Well, that was a close shave,' said Lathom.

He picked himself up and dusted himself down then he looked over and saw Sheryl cradling Melville in her arms. He was grimacing, obviously in pain and had his arm across his chest. Lathom could see blood oozing between his fingers.

'Here — let me see,' he knelt beside Melville and moved his arm. 'Phone an ambulance — now!'

'Don't worry, Bobby; he'll be fine. Just help me get him back to the apartment.'

'I don't care what you two have done. This is serious — I know plenty about gunshot wounds. If he doesn't get to hospital soon he's going to die.'

'Help me, and I'll explain everything — OK?'

Lathom reluctantly agreed, took off his scarf and put it over the wound. He told Melville to keep the pressure on it to stop the bleeding then they picked him up and, one on either side, walked him across the Strand and into the apartment block.

The young concierge was on duty.

'Evening Pete,' said Lathom, 'our friend here's had one too many. We're putting him to bed to let him sleep it off.'

'Any idea what that noise was?—it sounded like a gun.'

'Car back-firing, nothing to worry about.'

They dressed Melville's wounds and put him to bed. Lathom was surprised that the bleeding stopped so quickly and also that Melville didn't deteriorate, as he had first feared. Sheryl switched off the main light, leaving on only the bedside light, and kissed Melville on the forehead.

'Sleep tight,' she whispered.

Lathom went into the lounge and sat on the sofa while Sheryl rummaged under the sink in the kitchen for Melville's precious Irish whiskey and two glasses.

'I think you'll need some of this,' she said.

'Listen,' said Lathom. 'I don't care what you've done; I can help you. I've still got contacts—he needs to go to hospital.'

She reached out and touched his cheek. 'Don't worry, Bobby, we can look after ourselves—honestly. We've had plenty of practice. Just keep out of the way and we'll make sure you're safe—OK?'

'You don't get it, Sheryl. I spent my life thinking I was doing bad things to bad people for a good cause, then I realised that the bad people were exactly the same as me. Only, to them I was the bad person and their cause was the good one. When you're in a trench being shot at, you don't fight for king or country, a cap badge or even a flag; you fight for the friend standing by your side. Lee took that bullet for me and that's why I'm in the trench with you both.'

'That's a lovely speech, Bobby, but it's more complicated than that. Pour yourself a large whiskey, you'll need it.'

Two large whiskeys later and Sheryl had finished speaking. Lathom sat in silence.

'I knew you wouldn't believe me.' She went to put the whiskey away.

'Wait,' Lathom stood up and left the apartment. A few minutes later he returned with a book.

'So, let's get this straight,' he said, sitting down again. 'You, Lee and Kelly are vampires. He killed Kelly, Kelly killed you and some woman called Isabella killed Lee?'

'Yes.'

'Now, Kelly wants revenge. He wants to chop you up and keep you in suitcase, and do something even nastier to Lee?'

'Yes, —I said you wouldn't believe me.'

'Did I say I don't believe you? But you could be mad or I might have concussion. If it's true then there will be some proof, won't there?'

'Suppose so. Can't think what.'

'You said Lee was here in 1914, and was a Captain in the army. What name did he use then?'

'Melville, —I think.'

Lathom picked up his book, checked the index and placed the book open on the coffee table where Sheryl could see a black and white portrait of a young man in military uniform. The hair was much shorter and he had a neatly trimmed moustache, but the young man was unmistakably Lee and the caption read: 'Captain Stanley Richard Melville VC'.

The following morning, after a sleepless night, Lathom knocked at Sheryl's apartment. The door opened and Sheryl peered out and checked the corridor.

'Oh, Hello Mister Lathom. How can I help you?' she said smiling.

'Funny?' Lathom grunted.

'What's the matter with you Bobby?'

'Too much of Lee's whiskey and not enough sleep. How is he today?'

'Much better. He's propped up in bed like the lord of the manor and I'm doin' me best Florence Nightingale impersonation. Better not mention the whiskey; he'll only get arsey.'

'It might be a good idea if we moved him into my apartment. They know where you live and they might come back anytime.'

'You sure?'

'Get his things and we'll move him across.'

Once Sheryl and Melville were settled in his apartment Lathom collected his car from the resident's car park. He found it difficult to believe everything he'd been told. If Sheryl's account was true, then it was possible that he could have met Kelly years before their meeting on the pier. It was such a crazy idea; it needed corroboration — and there was only one person he could ask. He drove along the dock road, north out of the city and turned down a small cobbled street. At the far end there was a small shabby pub. After driving round the block to check that he wasn't being followed, he parked in an adjacent street opposite a disused dock. He was wearing his steel toe-capped boots and had one of his 'Chow Mein' specials in his pocket except that, at the last moment, he decided to place the gun under the driver's seat together with the car keys. Arriving armed would set the wrong tone for the coming encounter. He left the car unlocked; he might still need to make a quick getaway.

The outside of the pub was dismal with peeling paint and a large, tatty banner that advertised 'SKY- Sports'. The name over the door was Daniel Francis Corcoran, licensed to sell beers wines and spirits. Lathom took a deep breath and entered.

'Afternoon Sir, what can I get you?' said the landlord and then he recognised Lathom, 'You've a fucking cheek coming here, you bastard. Get back under your fucking stone!'

'So nice to see you too, Danny.'

'Fuck off before I do something I'll regret.'

Lathom heard a chair being pushed back behind him.

'What's the matter, Danny? This fat arsehole bothering you?' said a voice.

'Call him off,' said Lathom without looking round, 'or I'll have to hurt him.'

'Don't worry Liam. Just an old friend, nothin' to worry about,' said Danny.

'No need to get excited Danny. It's only a social call.'

'Like your last one? Half a dozen bizzies with pick-axe handles, smashing up me pub and breaking four of me ribs?'

'Sorry.'

'Don't give me any of that shit.'

'I mean — sorry I meant to break your legs as well.'

'Always the joker, Bob? What d'yer want?'

'A favour.'

'Well you always had balls; I'll give you that.'

'It's about Billy Flanagan.'

'I had nothin' to do with that.'

'I know, but you know who did — don't you?'

A barmaid came behind the bar from the saloon where she'd been cleaning tables.

'Going for a smoke, Bernie,' Danny told her. 'Call me if yer get busy.'

He showed Lathom to an upstairs room that was as shabby as the bar. There was a sink full of dirty dishes, and two threadbare arm chairs sat in front of a dusty TV separated by a low table with an ashtray full of dog ends. Lathom moved a take-away box from the chair and sat down while Danny rummaged in the sink and placed two grubby glasses on the table. He produced a bottle from behind the TV. He showed it to Lathom who nodded appreciatively.

'Keep the good stuff up 'ere,' he said and poured two generous glasses before taking out a cigarette and offering the pack to Lathom.

'No thanks, I've given up.'

'It's a fucked up world, Bob.' Danny waved his cigarette and sat down opposite. 'Can't even smoke in me own pub anymore.'

Lathom studied him. He'd put on a lot of weight since they last met, his face was red and puffy and he wheezed slightly. They'd both been young men back then; now they were a couple of old war horses waiting for the knacker's yard.

'Tell me who killed Flanagan.'

'Why — its thirty years ago?'

'Nearer forty.'

'Exactly—so why does it matter? Too many died, Bob, and all for nothin'

'But not like that: sliced up, mutilated, hung on a hook like a piece of meat.'

'I had nothin' to do with it; you know that. You tried hard enough to get me to talk back then. And if getting a good kicking from the bizzies, then fallin' down the stairs at that fuckin' Bridewell didn't loosen me tongue, what makes you think I'll tell you over a glass of me own whiskey?'

'Because, as you said, it was long ago and everyone involved is probably dead.' Lathom reached into his coat and took out an old photograph. 'This him?'

'Why's e' in fucking fancy dress?'

'Perhaps he was auditioning for 'Gone with the wind."

'Always the joker Bob? I'm saying nothin'. Never been a grass, never will be. Drink your drink then fuck off.'

'You knew Flanagan—he didn't deserve to die like that, did he? It didn't help *the cause*, did it? Whoever killed him was a sick bastard.'

'I'm saying nothin'. The man who did it was a mad bastard; everyone was frightened of him; even the 'provos' left him well alone.'

'Tell me!—Is this him?' Lathom thrust the photo under Danny's nose and, finally, Danny nodded, almost imperceptibly.

'I need a name,' said Lathom.

Danny shook his head. 'I'm saying nothin'. I won't grass up no one, specially a mad bastard like that.'

'Was it Steve Kelly?'

Danny went white and stared ahead.

'Thanks,' said Lathom.

'For what? I didn't say owt. Did I?'

Lathom raised his glass and toasted, 'absent friends.'

Danny repeated the toast, then added, 'Now fuck off.'

Lathom felt he needed one final piece of evidence before he could accept what Sheryl had told him. He went back to his car and called an old friend at the department — he needed to know if it was possible he'd met Kelly many years before.

An hour later his phone rang and a voice he didn't recognise repeated a number to him twice, waited for him to repeat it and then hung up. He wrote it down in Richardson's old address book, for some reason he hadn't disposed of it, even though it linked him to his murder.

Within ten minutes he was standing in Rumford Court in front of Kelly's flat. When he was last there he had been convinced that Kelly was dead; now he wasn't so sure. He turned the key and pushed the door open. Closing the door quietly behind him, he paused and listened intently. He waited for what seemed an eternity but heard nothing then he took the 'Chow Mein' special from his pocket and screwed on the bulky silencer. It was better to be safe than sorry. He worked methodically from room to room. The flat was unoccupied but there was evidence that someone was living here. He needed to find his proof then leave before that someone returned. It would be best if no one was aware of his visit.

He took down the oil painting of the *CSS Florida* and opened the wall-safe. Whoever lived there was obviously unaware that he had visited before because the combination was unchanged. The $17000 was missing but Kelly's passport, the access codes and the gun were still inside. He took out the Browning automatic and checked the serial number against the number in Richardson's address book. They matched — this was Flanagan's missing gun. He replaced it and locked the safe, then slipped quietly out of the flat. Walking back towards his car, the full impact of what he had discover was beginning to sink in. He had thought that he was going mad, but now he knew he was sane.

He was just in the middle of a vendetta between vampires. Perhaps retirement wouldn't be so boring after all.

When he opened the door to his apartment he smelled food cooking and, in the lounge, Sheryl was sitting on the sofa painting her nails.

'Hi Florence. How's his lordship?'

'Hasn't stopped complaining, so he must be on the mend. Where've you been? I was beginning to think you'd done a runner.'

'Been to see an old enemy about our mutual friend.'

'Who?'

'Kelly.'

'And?'

'I believe your story. I may be mad and only think I'm sane, but we'll worry about that later. First things first — how do we kill the bastard?'

'Get those clodhoppers off your feet and get your slippers on; you should never plan a murder on an empty stomach.'

He went to hang his coat on the back of a chair and noticed the old photograph in his pocket. He unfolded it. It was a full-length portrait of a fair-haired man in Confederate army uniform, complete with sabre and waxed moustache. He took the photo album he'd found in the safety-deposit box down from his bookcase and carefully replaced the photograph on the page marked 'Birmingham Alabama 1862'.

Sheryl and Lathom ate together while Melville slept in Lathom's bedroom.

'He's a brave man,' said Lathom as he pushed his empty plate to one side.

'Who?'

'Lee!'

'Oy! You cheeky sod my food isn't that bad!' she laughed and punched his arm.

'You know what I mean,' said Lathom, '- you don't get the VC for nothing.'

'Yes but don't mention it; his head's big enough as it is.'

Lathom went to his study and returned a few moments later with a parcel which he passed to Sheryl. She unwrapped it and there was the Webley and a bundle of letters tied with a red ribbon.

'He used that gun when he won the VC,' said Lathom, 'and those are love letters from someone called Charlotte. I don't feel comfortable keeping either of them now I know him.'

Sheryl untied the ribbon, sat down on the sofa began to read the letters.

'Do you think you should do that?' asked Lathom.

'I already know about her—but if I read her words I may understand what happened between them.'

Lathom went back to his study to collect a new bottle of single malt. He poured two glasses and handed one to Sheryl, muttering to himself, 'I think it's going to be another long night.'

The following morning he woke with a pounding headache and nearly fell off the sofa.

'Here, drink this.'

He saw a blurred Sheryl looking down at him, holding a glass of water with a tablet fizzing in it. He sat up with difficulty and took it from her then realised that he was fully clothed and had a blanket wrapped around him.

'How did I -?'

'You fell asleep and I didn't want you to get cold.'

Lathom noticed the empty bottle on the coffee table, groaned and hesitantly drank the fizzy water.

'Do you feel as bad as me?' he asked.

'No, Bobby, I feel fine. Don't get *those* sort of hangovers any longer.'

'How's Lee?'

'Much better. Come and see him when you feel up to it,' she pointed to the Webley on the table and added, 'I think it would be nice if *you* gave that to him.'

Later that morning, and still feeling delicate, Lathom went through to see Lee, who was sitting up in bed and seemed more like someone with a cold than the victim of a fatal gunshot wound received less than two days before.

'Just wanted to thank you for what you did.'

Melville looked embarrassed.

'Sheryl's told me your secret — and about Kelly,' continued Lathom.

Melville's eyes turned towards Sheryl who sat beside him on the bed. She nodded and took hold of his hand.

'I'd like to return something you once owned,' said Lathom and handed over the Webley. Melville held it and ran his fingers over its surface, then sat silently as if deep in thought. Finally he handed it back to Lathom.

'It's yours now, Bob. That was a different time, a different life. We should leave the past dead and buried.'

'There's something else,' said Sheryl and handed him the letters.

Lathom took his leave and slipped away.

Now that he knew that Kelly was a vampire Lathom's thoughts turned to the items he'd found in the safety-deposit box. He now knew that the photo album was Kelly's and since the gun and watch were of a similar age, perhaps they were his too. He decided to retrieve them from the bank vault to see if Melville knew anything of their history. When he returned Sheryl was back in the kitchen and Lee was resting.

'Everything OK?' he asked.

'Yeah, fine — I know everything now. I'll tell you later — but don't mention it to Lee.'

'Course not — none of my business anyway. I've been to get some things that I know belong to Kelly. I thought Lee might know something about them.'

Lathom opened a large jiffy bag and put the gun and watch on the table. Sheryl, smiled, picked up the gun, pointed it at him and pulled back the hammer.

'It's like a cowboy's gun,' she said. 'Is it loaded?'

'No. It's called a 'Navy' Colt; it's from the Civil War.'

'You got any bullets?'

'Doesn't take bullets; it's too old for that. It's a ball and powder gun. You load the six chambers one at a time. Black powder first then wading, then tamp down a small lead ball on top. You fire it with a percussion cap that you push on the back of each chamber — here.' He pointed at the back of the revolver.'

'Sounds complicated, Bobby—so it's useless then?'

'You could still use it. Just takes time to load it.'

'But you said you can't get bullets for it anymore.'

'You can get gunpowder and you can make the lead balls easily enough.'

'Can you?'

Lathom nodded, went to his study and returned with a small wooden box. It contained what looked like a perfume bottle and several small tins containing lead balls, wading and percussion caps. Taking the gun from her, he tipped the bottle into one of the chambers and poured a measured amount of black powder, placed a small piece of wading on top of it, pushing it down gently, then selected a small lead ball from one of the tins and dropped it into the chamber packing it down firmly to stop it falling out.

'Will it fire now?'

'Not without the percussion cap—but there's no safety catch on these old guns, so best not.'

'Go on, I'll be careful, honest.'

'Just don't point it at me—OK?'

He fitted a percussion cap then rotated the chamber until it was in the 6 o'clock position directly opposite the firing pin at 12 o'clock.

'It's safe unless you turn the chamber—OK?'

Sheryl took the gun from him, spun the chamber and pulled back the hammer.

'Careful!' he shouted.

'Always fancied meself as Jesse James.' She twirled the gun around her finger. 'Hey, Bobby,—let's find a bank to rob.'

'Umm — perhaps not,' he carefully took the gun from her, '- this is only going end in tears.' He rotated the chamber back to the safe position.

'Don't be so borin'.' She pulled a face like a petulant child.

'Better boring than dead.' He put the gun back in the jiffy bag and threw the watch to her. 'Play with that if you like.'

She caught the watch and dangled it from its gold chain. 'This Kelly's too?'

'Not sure. It's got a dedication inside if you look.'

'Oh yeah 'from a Sarah-Jane to her beloved James'.'

'It must be a trophy. Somehow I can't imagine our Mr Kelly being anyone's beloved James, can you? Wonder who it belonged to?'

'Perhaps Lee will know. We can ask him later. Where did you get all this stuff from anyway?'

'From Kelly's safety-deposit box.'

'How?'

'An old friend mine called Richardson had the key.'

'And what happened to him?'

'I killed him.'

'I thought you killed Kelly?'

'I did — and Richardson too.'

'Why?'

'Richardson tricked me into killing Kelly for him and then didn't pay up. In fact, he sent some thugs to kill me instead.'

'What happened to them? Don't tell me — you killed them too?'

Lathom nodded.

'How many of them?'

'Four.'

'Jesus Bobby. You having a one man war or do you just enjoy it?'

'Just business, nothing personal.'

'Hate to see you when it gets personal!' Sheryl laughed.

'What about you and Lee?'

'What about us, Bobby?'

'Do you enjoy it — the killing?'

'Lee feels guilty about it. He tries not to do it but he always relapses in the end.'

'And you?'

'It's just what I do. Some people need to gamble, some need drugs — I need blood. Simple as that.'

She handed the watch back to Lathom who put it back in the jiffy bag. She seemed keen to change the subject.

'Well, Bobby — what are you doing tonight?'

'Nothing really — thought I'd do a bit on my book.'

'Great you can come to the fancy dress party with me — I've got a spare ticket now.'

'You're still planning to go — after all this?'

'Why not? It'll be a laugh.'

'What about Kelly?'

'I don't think he's invited. You've got to come; I had a great outfit for Lee but I wouldn't put it passed him to have got shot on purpose just to get out of going.'

'Well, I'd love to come — but I really haven't got anything to wear.'

'I thought that what women were supposed to say? Pity Lee's costume won't fit you.'

'Sorry.'

'Look, it's dead easy- you keep an eye on his lordship, and I'll pop into town and get something for you. Go on Bobby — say you'll come?–It's for a good cause.'

'What the donkey sanctuary again?'

'No Bobby — one even closer to my heart — blood donors! They say — 'You may need blood one day.' well I do every day Bobby.'

A few hours later Sheryl returned carrying several bags and in high spirits.

'I got a great blouse and a head scarf from the charity shop off Williamson Square — earrings from the Market and a belt from a vintage shop in Bold Street.'

'I'm not dressing as a woman — no way.'

'Don't worry, you're a pirate — Captain Bobby.'

'And you?'

'You put these on and I'll go and change.'

Lathom smiled as he sorted through the bag. He put on the frilly white blouse, tied the polka-dot headscarf as a bandana and clipped the large hoop earring on one ear. The wide leather belt completed the effect. As added insurance, just in case Kelly gate-crashed the party, he went to his study and retrieved his cutlass. He was just admiring himself in a mirror when Sheryl returned; she was wearing a skin-tight, sequined dress and a curly blonde wig.

'Ta dah!' she struck a theatrical pose, 'guess who?'

'Dolly Parton?'

'No — Marilyn Munroe!'

'Yes — of course ...'

'We'd better get a move on Bobby. I don't want to miss out on buying a raffle ticket. Who knows — first prize might be a year's supply of blood.'

– 5 –

Pier Head

It was after midnight when Peter reached the apartment block. He stood in Chavasse Park for a while and tried to clear his head. What was he doing here? Was he mad? How could he make them believe him — if even he couldn't believe it? Natasha had been abducted by a maniac who threatened to kill her if he didn't do exactly what he told him to do and he was risking her life on the word of a parrot.

The more he thought about it, the more ludicrous it seemed, but, ludicrous or not, it appeared that her only hope was for him to warn them tonight. He looked up at the 13th Floor which was all in darkness. Perhaps they were asleep? How could he check if they were there? He would call from the reception desk then pretend it was a wrong number. He wasn't working until 7am so he needed an excuse for being so early and he couldn't just go up to 13C because the concierge on duty would see him on the CCTV monitor screen and might call security. Peter didn't know what to do, but he knew that he couldn't wait in the park for seven hours and that he wouldn't go home now. He walked into the main entrance; luckily Phil was manning the desk that night.

'Hiya Pete. What you doin' 'ere so early?' Phil looked up from his book and smiled. 'Not 'ad a domestic with the lovely Natasha 'ave yer?'

Peter gratefully seized on the idea. 'That's about right—threw me out, and I can't face going back to my room. Do you mind if I stop for a bit?'

'Sit yerself down. I'll get yer a coffee—one sugar isn't it?'

While Phil went into the back room and switched on the kettle, Peter buzzed 13C and the sound of the water boiling hid the noise of the buzzer. He held the button-down for a long time, but there was no answer. They must still be out—what if they didn't come back in time, would the man in black, Kelly, still kill Natasha? It seemed certain that he would. Her only hope was the couple in 13C and Peter would have to wait for them to return. He played with the master-key in his pocket and came to a sudden decision.

'Don't worry about the coffee Phil,' he called out. 'See you in the morning.' Then he quickly took the lift to the 13th Floor before Phil returned.

They tumbled out of the lift laughing and Lathom fumbled for his key.

'Lee should've come; it was such a laugh,' Sheryl giggled, 'especially when you threatened that guy with your sword because he thought you were a gypsy fortune teller.'

'We pirates are touchy about things like that.'

'You seemed to be getting on well with Cleopatra. You spent most of the evening looking down her cleavage. What were you doing Bobby—looking for her asp?'

'Hey!—what about you and that DJ?'

'Don't tell Lee—he gets dead jealous.'

They walked the sort distance down the corridor to Lathom's apartment and he was about to put his key in the lock when Sheryl noticed light coming from under the door of 13C opposite.

'Bobby look!' she whispered.

Their jovial mood evaporated. They stared at the light patch on the carpet

'Do you think Lee has gone back to your apartment?' asked Lathom.

'Doubt it. He was tucked up in bed when I left him — reading one of your books.'

'Do you think it's Kelly?' Lathom drew his cutlass.

'Let's get Lee first — before we do anything.'

'You sure he's up to it?'

'I told you Bobby he's fine now — just swinging the lead to get out of wearing fancy dress.'

A few minutes later they were standing in front of the door to 13C. Sheryl and Lathom in fancy dress and Melville in his dressing gown and slippers.

Melville took his key and quietly unlocked the door. They waited anxiously expecting something to happen but, when nothing did, he slowly pushed the door open. Lathom drew his cutlass and pushed past them. He crept down the short entrance hall towards the lounge. Melville looked at Sheryl and shrugged and they followed. Lathom peered around the edge of the lounge door.

He turned to them and whispered, 'Just one of them — let's rush him?'

Before they could answer he charged into the room waving his cutlass and screaming.

Peter had been asleep on the sofa. He was woken when a fat pirate with a very large sword ran into the room screaming. He screamed too and jumped behind the sofa for protection.

'Stop Bobby — it's only Pete from the desk.' Sheryl pulled Lathom back by his belt.

'Pete?' Lathom was disorientated, 'What you doing here, lad?'

'Waiting.'

'Why?' Sheryl asked.

'I've got a parcel for you — from a mad man.'

Sheryl nodded at Lathom who put the cutlass back in its scabbard.

'You boys sit down. I'll put the kettle on and Pete can tell us everything.'

'Any chance of a whisky?' asked Lathom.

'No Bobby -I think we all need clear heads.'

They sat on the L-shaped sofa, Lathom on one side of Peter and Melville on the other. When she returned with the mugs of tea, Sheryl squeezed between Peter and Melville.

'Now Pete,' she said, 'start at the beginning, and take it slowly.'

'It started today — my girlfriend and I had gone for a picnic and when we were on the way home we got separated and this man in black took her.'

'How do you know that?'

'He told me — said he'd kill her if I didn't give you this parcel tomorrow morning at 9 am.'

'Why didn't you look for her?'

'He had a gun — said if I tried anything he'd cut her up into pieces and post them to me.'

Sheryl and Melville exchanged a look.

'He said it was important that I gave it to you tomorrow, 9 am no earlier — or he'd hurt her.'

'Why have you come here now? Why not wait?'

'Frank told me to come — he said you'd know what to

do. He said this man would kill her anyway, whatever happens and only you could help her.

'Where's this Frank now?'

'He flew off.'

'Sorry?'

'He changed his wings because he said that he had a lot of ground to cover tonight.'

'*Wings?*'

'He's a seagull now. He used to be pigeon but they've only got little wings.'

'He's a *seagull?* This Frank is a seagull?'

'Now — but he used to be a pigeon. Last time we talked it was about my wife's death and he was a pigeon then.'

Sheryl put her arm around his shoulder.

'Pete — I think it's just in your head, luv. Pigeons can't talk. You drink your tea and we'll call the doctor.'

'I know that — but Frank's not really a pigeon; he's an angel, my guardian angel.'

Sheryl looked at Melville and Lathom.

'Don't you worry, lad,' Lathom patted his knee, 'you'll soon be right as rain. A few pills from the Doc and a nice rest — do you the world of good.'

'I knew you wouldn't believe me; I told him so — but he said only you could help and that I was to tell you something and that would make you know it was true.'

'What?' Melville spoke for the first time.

'He said the man was called Kelly and he was a vampire.'

'Anything else?'

'Yes, — he died here in Liverpool in 1863.'

'Two,' said Melville, '-1862.'

'That's right 1862 — how did you know that?'

'I've a good memory.'

'You believe me then?'

'Let's see the parcel first—then I'll decide?'

Peter took the parcel from his pocket.

'I don't know what's in it? It could be someone's ear—I didn't want to look inside.'

Melville and Sheryl exchanged a look and Melville took the parcel from Peter.

'Why did you think it was for us?' asked Melville. 'It's addressed to 'the Lone Ranger and Tonto'?'

'I thought it must be a nick-name or something?—He said the couple in 13C.'

Melville held the parcel to his ear and shook it then Sheryl passed him her penknife and he carefully cut it open and emptied the contents onto the coffee table—a small mobile phone and two slips of paper.

'What if he calls?' said Sheryl. 'We're not supposed to have it until 9 am.'

Melville picked up the paper. 'Tickets for the Mersey cruise—10 am tomorrow. Now we know where—but why?' He switched on the phone. 'There's a message on this—now we find out why.'

He pressed the phone and held it to his ear and they sat in silence while he listened. Then he passed it to Sheryl and then to Lathom.

'What about me?' said Peter.

Lathom passed the phone back to Melville who switched it off and put it back in the jiffy bag.

'Not for your ears, lad,' said Lathom. 'You need some rest—busy day tomorrow. Come with me; you can sleep on my sofa.'

Peter tried to object but reluctantly agreed and went with Lathom. Melville and Sheryl sat in silence for a few moments

'Bastard!' she muttered.

'Probably,' said Melville.

'What are we going to do, Lee?'

'What he asks.'

'Why? He'll kill her anyway.'

'I know- but if we don't we'll always have to keep watching our backs. This way we may bring it all to a close once and for all.'

'Do you really think those things are all he wants — that he's given up wanting revenge on you?'

'No, but at least we've got –' Melville checked his watch, '- seven hours to prepare a plan. He's not expecting that; that's our ace in the hole.'

'You believe Pete's angel story?'

'Don't know?' He laughed. 'I didn't used to believe in vampires.'

Sheryl leaned over and kissed him: 'You're a good man Lee Melville.'

'I need to tell you something — in case anything happens.'

'I know, Lee — you love me.'

'No — well, yes — but not that. Something about the past, about when it all started.'

'About Emma?'

'You may not think I'm so good afterwards — but you need to know everything.'

'There's no need Lee — some things are best left in the past.'

Melville ignored her and began speaking, 'It was a few weeks after the battle of Waterloo.'

Sheryl moved closer to him on the sofa and took his hand in her's. 'OK—if it'll make you feel better.'

'It was a few weeks after the battle. I'd 'miraculously' survived a musket ball to the chest and had managed to arrange a pass to allow me to recuperate in Brussels. I went to visit Isabella to tell her of my lucky escape and it was then that she told me what she'd done—how she'd *made* me a vampire. Obviously I didn't believe her, but then she told me a little of her life and explained the reality of her existence—her loneliness—how she wanted a soul-mate to live with forever—and how she'd chosen me. I was still besotted with her and, whether I believed what she told me or not, at least it proved that she loved me. Then she explained that the only thing standing in the way of our eternal happiness was her husband; she had no money of her own and he would never allow her to leave.

I felt very confused by what she'd told me. The dreams had already started by this time and I was beginning to feel detached from reality. I was having nightmares and hallucinations during the day, and was wondering about my sanity—you know how it is.'

'Yes,' Sheryl squeezed his arm. 'You feel you're going mad.'

'But somehow what she said made sense—perfect sense.'

'She wanted you to kill him?'

Melville nodded, 'I wasn't a stranger to death.—I'd killed men before, but always in the heat of battle and never in cold blood.'

'Why hadn't she killed him herself?'

'She said she was too fond of him—but I later realised there was another reason.'

'Sneaky cow.'

'We made love and she explained her plan to me. She said that it would need to look like a robbery that had gone wrong so that neither of us would be suspected and so that she could inherit his money, then we would run away together — forever. The following evening, I was waiting in an alley on his usual route to his club with a scarf around my face and a sharp knife. She told me to make sure to take his purse; it always contained gold coins and would provide a motive for the murder.

I waited for what seemed like hours, my conscience battling with the weird hallucinations and the craving for blood. Many times I was about to leave but something kept me there — perhaps my love for her or maybe just the lust for blood. Then he appeared. Even with the scarf round my face he recognised me and was about to embrace me as a friend when I stabbed him — three times. I still remember the shocked look on his face as he fell to the ground. I searched his body and found the small leather purse but, as I was about to put it in my pocket — his maid arrived.

She was holding his gloves in her hand and had obviously been rushing to catch up with her master. She screamed when she saw me searching his body and when I looked up I saw that she recognised me. There was only one thing I could do otherwise I would lose Isabella forever; I grabbed her by the throat to silence her. When she fell to the ground I realised that I had stabbed her too. I cradled her in my arms horrified and begging her forgiveness as she bleed to death. Then another urge took over — the urge to taste her blood.'

'That's enough—I understand.'

'She was only a child and I drank her blood.'

'I know, Lee. Leave it now; you didn't know what you were doing.'

'But I did—and I enjoyed it.'

'What happened next?'

'I took the money to Isabella—there was no gold and only a few silver coins. I told her about the maid, Emma. I wanted to go back and see if she was still alive but Isabella said the girl was lazy and it would be easy to find another maid.'

'So why didn't you live happily ever after?'

'The elation of the kill had gone and I realised what I'd done—I'd killed a friend and a child. I also realised something else—that Isabella had sent Emma to find her master and take him his gloves.'

'Why would she do that?'

'So that I'd either be identified as his murderer or kill the child and be forever under her control. I left—she didn't seem too concerned.'

'What about 'soul mates'—forever?'

'I found out later that she already had her Russian Prince waiting in the wings—I think perhaps I was merely a means to an end.'

'Evil bitch.'

'She wished me well and said that she bore me no ill will, then she offered me the coins from her husband's purse—they seemed like thirty pieces of silver.'

Sheryl laughed, 'Is that why you don't like change—Soft lad?'

Melville gave a half smile and shrugged.

'You're a good man, Lee Melville.' Sheryl leaned over and kissed him on the cheek.

The sun was just beginning to rise, a faint orange glow on the horizon. Melville looked out at the city below.

'Perhaps if we can save Peter's girl it'll make up for Emma,' he said.

'I know one thing.'

'What's that?'

'You need to get changed—you can't go fighting vampires in your slippers.'

Melville laughed, 'And what about you Dolly?'

Sheryl gave him a filthy look and punched him on the arm. 'I'll sort you out later, you cheeky sod—Once we've sorted out Kelly.

By 6 am were all back in Melville's apartment. Peter had obviously had a sleepless night and was half asleep on the sofa and Lathom appeared to have had a night cap or two. Sheryl cooked a fried breakfast to little enthusiasm from the others.

'You can't go fighting vampires on an empty stomach,' she said. 'That's what me mam always used to say. You want mushrooms, Bobby?'

'What are we going to do, Lee?' Lathom asked. 'You can't just meet him on the boat with the things he asked for—you've got no guarantee he'll give the girl back.'

Melville and Sheryl exchanged a look; they knew the girl wasn't coming back.

'What do you suggest, Bob?'

'Take a decoy. I'll keep the real things. If he turns up you do a deal. Meet again on neutral territory and do an exchange.'

'So two bags the same, and you watching our backs?'

'Exactly — we can use the Webley and one of my photo albums for the decoy.'

'Won't he kill her if you try to trick him?' asked Peter who had woken up.

'You've got to trust us, Pete.' Sheryl put her hand on his shoulder, 'The only thing keeping her alive is the fact we have the things he wants. Once he gets those he'll kill her whatever.'

'Exactly,' said Lathom. 'We need to get him to agree to an exchange on our terms.'

Sheryl and Melville agreed but with little conviction.

'Pete you look like shite,' said Sheryl. 'Go and freshen up; you start work soon.'

Forty minutes later Peter was taking over from Phil in reception.

'Look at the state of you- where's your tie?' said Phil.

Peter mumbled something about forgetting it.

'You can 'av mine. What you been up too? Don't tell me — you and Natasha been making up 'av you? — Lucky sod.' Phil picked up his sandwich box and book. 'Dan's taking over at seven tonight. Try and stay awake will you? We don't want Grimes complaining about you again, do we?'

Kelly was angry, and when that happened he did one of two things: hurt someone or went fishing. This morning he was fishing and he had begun to feel calmer. He'd caught a few whiting and with any luck he'd get the chance to hurt someone later.

He was angry with Dean and Lewis, or Tweedle-dean and Tweedle-dumb as he preferred to think of them.

They'd manged to lose the Taser and the Glock, let the Malone girl get away and put her and Melville on their guard. Things were now much more difficult due to their incompetence, but what could you expect from untrained scum? Doyle and the boys would never have screwed it up, but then again they weren't perfect because they'd managed to get themselves killed once he wasn't around to look after them.

He saw his 4X4 approaching and slowly packed away his fishing gear. He wanted to draw as little attention to himself as possible. The car pulled alongside side him and they beeped the horn which to his surprise played 'Dixie'.

'Fucking amateurs!' thought Kelly.

As he walked up to the car. Dean opened the passenger window.

'Hiya Mr K — d'yer like the 'orn? We bought it special like.'

'No!' Kelly scowled and put his fishing bag in the boot.

'Thought yer'd like it — you bein' a Yank an' all?'

'I'm not a Yankee! — I'm from the South.'

The brothers exchanged a puzzled look as Kelly climbed into the rear seat behind them.

'OK, do you remember the plan?'

The both nodded. He regretted having to trust them but 'needs must' he thought; he couldn't do it alone and they were all he had.

'Lewis, you take the fishing gear and wait by the ferry terminal. Message me when they board the ferry then take the car through the tunnel and check that they don't get off at any of the stops. Message me after each stop — OK?'

Lewis nodded, 'Yeah, 'll text yer—like yer said Mr K.'

It seemed to Kelly that Lewis or Tweedle dumb was the weak link. That was why he'd given him a menial task that was unlikely to jeopardise the plan.

'Dean,' Kelly continued, '- you and I will wait until Tweedl... Lewis messages me. Then we'll go to the apartment.—Did you bring a box like I told you to?'

'Deffo Mr K—put the Uzi in it like yer said.'

'Good—don't use it unless absolutely necessary—OK? We don't want the police swarming all over the place do we?'

They both shook their heads. Kelly groaned, then tapped Lewis on the shoulder.

'Give Dean your knife.'

'Why?'

'In case he needs to deal with a problem—quietly.'

Lewis reluctantly handed over his knife. Kelly checked his watch and tapped him on the shoulder again.

'Take us to Chavasse Park then go and wait by the ferry terminal for them to arrive. Don't forget the messages—OK?'

Lewis grinned, 'No worries Mr K—yer can bank on me, like.'

It was nearly 9.45 am Melville checked the mobile and put it in his pocket. 'In case Kelly calls us on the ferry,' he explained. He was dressed in black as usual and Sheryl was still in her fancy dress, with a thick fur coat over the top, and her Russian hat covering the blonde wig. She squeezed his arm.

'Just like being in a 60's spy film, Lee—dead romantic. You be Sean Connery and I'll be Marilyn Munroe.'

'Can't we be ourselves?'

'God Lee, you're so borin'- make an effort.'

They left the apartment by the main entrance onto the Strand arm in arm, Melville carrying the duplicate jiffy bag containing the Webley and Lathom's photo album and walked the short distance to the Pier Head. Meanwhile, Lathom left by the side door into Chavasse Park and walked down the side steps onto the Strand so that he was some distance behind them and could check if they were being followed. He carried the jiffy bag containing Kelly's possessions and also had his 'Chow Mein' special with silencer so that he could intervene if they were ambushed on their way to the ferry.

Melville and Sheryl had the tickets from Kelly and stood by the railings at the top of the landing stage watching as the ferry pulled up alongside and the passengers disembarked. The new passengers boarded but there was no sign of Kelly or his thugs. They waited until the ferry was about to leave then ran down the walkway and up the gangplank at the last possible minute. Lathom stood hidden behind the wall of the terminal building. A small group of tourists were clustered in front of him taking photos of the ferry's departure while over the far side a man, who was carrying fishing gear, leaned on the railing smoking a cigarette. As the ferry pulled away, this man took a phone from his pocket appeared to send a text then turned and walked away from the terminal. There was something about him; Lathom followed.

The man approached a large American 4X4, parked next to the Liver Building. He took off his coat and Lathom recognised him as the smaller of the two men who had tried to abduct Sheryl and the car as the one he had seen in Rumford Court when he'd originally searched Kelly's apartment. The man drove off.

'Amateurs,' thought Lathom and sent a text, then he tucked the jiffy bag under his arm and walked slowly back towards the apartment building.

It was just after 10am. Kelly and Dean were waiting in the underground car park underneath Chavasse Park which was four stories above them. Kelly had the Browning in his coat and his razor in his boot. Dean had Lewis's knife in his pocket and carried the Uzi inside a small cardboard box. Kelly handed him a red baseball cap.

'You're a courier with a parcel — OK?'

Dean grinned, 'No sweat, Mr K, piece of piss.'

Kelly was about to say something when his phone beeped. He read Lewis's text then they walked the short distance to the main entrance of the apartment block. Dean pulled on the cap and pressed the intercom button; a voice crackled.

'Hello?'

'Parcel — need a signature.' Dean smiled at Kelly who scowled at him.

The door buzzed and unlocked and Dean entered with his parcel, Kelly following closely behind. Peter, the concierge, stood up to sign for the parcel and Kelly hit him from behind with his gun. They gaffer-taped his hands and feet together, taped his mouth and locked him in the small staff room. Kelly had decided not to kill him immediately in case they needed another hostage — but if things went well he could kill him on the way out so there were no witnesses. He fully intended to kill the girl later once he'd had some fun with her; he had no intention of keeping his part of the bargain with Melville if he could avoid it.

Taking the master-key from behind the desk Kelly and Dean called both lifts and each took a separate lift to the 13th floor. They also took the two large ornamental pot plants from reception and used these to hold the doors open and keep the lifts trapped there after they arrived. Kelly had isolated the floor and now had little chance of being interrupted. At this time of day most of the residents would be at work. As a precaution, he left Dean in the corridor with the machine-gun.

Kelly checked his watch. Melville and Malone would be away at least fifty minutes and, once they were on the ferry, they couldn't change his mind. They would have to take the complete trip and that would give Kelly plenty of time to search the apartment. If he was lucky he might even find his possessions here — then he could definitely keep the girl as well.

He quietly opened the door to 13C with the master-key and, holding Flanagan's gun in his left hand, quickly checked that the apartment was empty. Satisfied, he started a methodical search, looking first for his possessions and, when that was unsuccessful, for any clues to their whereabouts. He was sure that Melville wouldn't have been naïve enough to take them with him. They wouldn't worry if he killed the girl or not, that threat was just to get the concierge to do what he wanted. Melville would want to meet to try to make a deal, the girl was expendable.

Melville and Sheryl watched as the crew on the landing stage pulled up the gangplank, the engines churned away in the bowel of the ship holding its position against the fast flowing Mersey, men undid the hawsers from the quayside and the ferry pulled away.

A speaker crackled into life and a recorded announcement described the itinerary of the 'River Explorer Cruise'. They would first sail up the Mersey toward the mouth of the river, then cross over and sail down the opposite bank, passing New Brighton and reaching their first stop at Seacombe Ferry Terminal in approximately twenty minutes. Passengers would be free to leave or join the ferry there or stay on board and travel on to Woodside Ferry Terminal ten minutes further on. From Woodside the ferry would return to the Pier Head, which would take a further twenty minutes. The announcement cut off and was replaced by a recording of 'Ferry 'cross the Mersey'. Melville laughed and Sheryl scowled.

'I hate this bleeding song,' she said. 'It always makes me cry.'

'Why?'

'When I was away it made me feel homesick,' she dabbed her eye with a tissue.

'But you're home now.'

'Now it makes me think about the life I lost.'

He put his arm around her and hugged her. 'What about the one you've found?' he asked.

She sniffed and blew her nose. 'Come on, Soft lad. No time for that—we've got a rendezvous with a psycho.'

They searched the ship but there was no sign of Kelly then Melville's phone buzzed. He read the text from Lathom.

'Bob says one of Kelly's thugs, watched us sail off,' Melville read. 'He sent a message to someone then drove off in an American 4X4.'

'Perhaps Kelly will get on at Seacombe,' Sheryl suggested.

They sat on the top deck; it was sunny but there was a cold wind. 'Glad you made me wear me hat and coat, Lee. It's bleeding freezing.'

Fifteen minutes later they were nearing their first stop. Sheryl was bored, she stood up leaned on the rail and stared at the approaching jetty at Seacombe.

'Lee! Come here and look. There's a big 4X4 parked by the quayside. Phone Bobby and ask what colour Kelly's was?'

Melville dialled the number.

'He's not answering.'

'The signal's dodgy in his apartment; try phoning Pete and ask him to call Bobby on the intercom.'

Melville dialled again. 'It's just ringing and ringing; perhaps Pete's checking something.'

'I don't like it Lee — you don't think this is a trick, do you?'

The ferry pulled alongside the quayside and the gangplank was lowered. Some passengers left and a few boarded but there was no sign of Kelly.

'Lee! It's definitely the shorter of those two scallies in the 4X4 so it must be Kelly's — but it doesn't look as though he's going to get on the ferry.'

There was a loud blast on the ferry foghorn to announce its departure. Melville was still on his phone. 'There's still no answer from reception.'

The gangplank was starting to be raised. Sheryl started taking off her coat and hat.

'What are you doing? I thought you were cold?'

'Gotta go, Lee — see you back home.'

She handed him her coat and hat, rummaged in the coat pocket, pulled out her penknife and tucked it down her cleavage then handed him her shoes.

'What're you doing?'

The gangplank had reached 45degrees and the engines were straining against the tide. She hitched up her dress.

'Hunting, Lee — that's what I'm doing,' she winked, 'Glad I wore me knickers.'

She ran towards the rail, vaulted onto the gangplank and ran down the other side. Melville looked down from the ship's the rail. She stood on the quayside looking up.

'Oy! Soft lad — shoes?'

He threw the shoes to her, she blew him a kiss and ran up the walkway towards the 4x4.

Lathom had just left the small supermarket on the Strand with another bottle of whisky. He knew he really should try to cut down on his alcohol consumption but right now it was the only thing that stopped the dreams. He felt a little shaky this morning and a small glass or two would soon stop that — or so he hoped. He intended to go back to his apartment and wait for Sheryl and Lee to either return — or to text him to bring the jiffy bag somewhere.

He opened the door to the block with his key-fob and expected to see Peter sitting behind the desk but it was empty. Some sixth sense made Lathom uneasy and he gripped his gun tighter and slowly checked reception before he called a lift. He tried the staffroom door but it was locked. He waited and waited but neither lift arrived and he became certain that something suspicious was going on. Should he call Lee? What was the point they were stuck on a ferry? He needed to act now.

Kelly and his thugs must be searching Lee and Sheryl's apartment while they were out. 'Sneaky bastard' thought Lathom with slight admiration.

However, Kelly obviously didn't realise who Lathom was nor his connection with Melville and that gave Lathom the element of surprise. His first task was to get to the 13th floor without the lifts and he definitely wasn't going to use the emergency stairs in his state; he wouldn't get halfway before either he had a heart attack or they would have long gone. He didn't mind losing his life in a gun fight but drew the line at dying of a cardiac arrest in a stairwell. He remembered that the lifts on the other side of the block went to the 10th floor and that there were emergency stairs for both sides of the block. If he took the lifts to the 10th he'd only have to walk down the corridor to the stairs on the other side and up three floors. He went outside and re-entered through the side door, took the lift to the 10th floor and was soon out of breath and crouching behind the fire door on the 13th floor. He took a sip of his whisky from his carrier bag and waited until he got his breath back, then he stood up slowly and looked through the small pane of safety glass in the fire door.

The taller of Kelly's thugs was leaning on the wall of a lift opposite under a *No Smoking* sign lighting a cigarette a machine-gun on the floor beside him. Well, they said smoking caused premature death, thought Lathom. He took the 'Chow Mein' special with its silencer from his coat, clicked off the safety catch and, taking a deep breath, pushed open the door with his left arm and extended his right arm in one fluid movement. The man reached for his machine-gun. There was a single, small 'thud' and he toppled forward on top of a large pot plant that held the door open.

Kelly must be in 13C and Lathom knew that he had to act quickly. He remembered what Sheryl had told him about vampires and that he still had the Taser in his apartment. He let himself into his own apartment, grabbed the Taser and handcuffs and went to the door of 13C, rummaging in his pocket for the spare key that Sheryl had given him. However the door was slightly ajar. He pushed it gently and crept inside. There were noises coming from the bedroom. Holding the Taser in his right hand and gun in his left and keeping close to the wall, he worked his way slowly down the corridor towards the source of the noises. When he reached the door to the bedroom, he took a deep breath then barged in.

Kelly turned. 'What the f... ?' he began to say, then the Taser hit him.

Lathom waited until the Taser stopped then handcuffed the semi-conscious man and propped him on a leopard-print armchair. Kelly was much as he remembered him. He had lost his hat when he fell and Lathom noticed that, since their meeting on the pier, he had lost the tip of his right ear and that the right side of his face was disfigured by a large burn.

Kelly regained consciousness and after swearing and struggling for a while realised his situation and calmed down. He looked at Lathom and smiled his crocodile smile.

'Hello Mr Davies,' he said, 'so good to see you again. I'd shake hands with you if you'd take these off.'

He was still wearing his dark glasses but Lathom remembered the cold eyes. He didn't reply.

'Cat got you tongue? Now there's an idea.' Kelly smiled, he wasn't worried, he still felt in control. 'You going to sit here in silence until the Long Ranger and Tonto come back from their cruise? You could at least tell me why you shot me?'

'I was paid to do it.'

'By who?'

'Richardson.'

'I must have underestimated him,' said Kelly. 'He say why?'

'No.' Lathom sat down on the bed.

'Then you killed him? Why?'

'He didn't pay up and he sent your thugs to kill me.'

'He was always a cheapskate,' Kelly muttered. 'And you killed Doyle and the boys?'

'Nothing personal then — not like you and Lee — just business.'

'I'm impressed. So, one business man to another: how much would it cost to set me free?'

'Sorry, it's personal now.'

'Why — because of the Dynamic Duo?'

'Because of Billy Flanagan.'

'Flanagan?' Kelly looked puzzled.

Lathom held up the Browning automatic he'd taken from Kelly's coat pocket.

'Flanagan was the man who owned this gun, the man you hung on a hook like a piece of meat. You slit his throat then cut out his heart and left it next to his warrant card.'

'Oh him. Called himself Flanagan then did he? I always think of him as O'Neil.'

This was getting strange. The conversation was absurdly matter-of-fact given Kelly's circumstances.

'Why O'Neil?' Lathom asked.

'That was his name — well, it was when I first met him.'

'First met him?' Lathom was confused.

'Here in 1862. He was my first and, like all of us, he seemed to resent it—like me and the Lone Ranger, or Tonto—I'm sure you get the idea. You'd think we'd be grateful wouldn't you—but no one ever is'

Lathom felt his headache coming back.

'Haven't you worked it out yet?' Kelly continued. 'Flanagan was a vampire too. He came looking for me. If I hadn't cut out his heart, he'd have done it to me.'

'Why?'

'We're difficult to kill and there aren't too many options. You can drain away every drop of blood but that takes time and it's not fool proof—or you can try removing a vital organ, the heart for example. There's beheading of course, or an explosion. Also you can try a combination of one or more ways to be certain—but you need to be careful and do the job properly or we'll only come back again in a *really* bad mood.'

'I can't tell if you're telling the truth or lying.' Lathom snatched the dark glasses from Kelly's face and then grimaced. The burn extended across the whole right side of his face stopping just short of his nose. The empty eye socket was a surprise.

'Satisfied?' Kelly asked. 'This is what your friends did to me, tried to blow me up with a booby trap. I lost an eye and -.' He was about to say more but changed his mind.

'Sorry.'

'Don't be. We're all the same. There's no good vampires; we all kill innocent people—not just to survive but because we enjoy it.'

'But—?'

'Don't be fooled by Tonto. You think she's pretty and fun? A victim of circumstance even? Next time, ignore the 'Jolly Scouser' act and look into her eyes.'

Lathom needed a drink but he'd left his whisky in his apartment and didn't want to take any of Lee's. Kelly smiled to himself. He could see that he'd sowed the seeds of doubt in Lathom's mind. Lathom looked confused and unsure of himself for once; he was no longer the calm killer on the pier.

'Come on, let's make a deal. Take these off so I can go to the john?' Kelly wriggled his cuffed hands behind his back.

'John?'

'Rest room — toilet.'

'No.'

But Lathom was unsure what to do. Perhaps Kelly was right and he'd only had half the story from Sheryl. What if everything she'd told him about Kelly had been lies? Perhaps they'd kill him once they no longer had any use for him? Lathom felt out of his depth and confused.

'She's going to be angry when I piss on her arm chair,' said Kelly. 'You don't want to see her angry.'

'Shut up!' Lathom grabbed Kelly by the shoulder and pushed him towards the en-suite. 'Just be quick.'

'You'll have to unlock them — unless you'd like to hold it for me,' said Kelly.

Lathom was drunk and disorientated but not stupid. He had Kelly lay face-down on the floor and held the gun to his head while he unlocked the cuffs, then he relocked one of the cuffs on his ankle. He knew from experience that a head shot wouldn't kill Kelly but it would incapacitate him for a while. Kelly lay passively and allowed himself to be cuffed; he didn't want to be shot again. Last time he'd had a headache for three weeks afterwards and, anyway, he already had a plan.

Kelly walked like a monkey into the en-suite. Lathom closed the door and took the opportunity to go back to his apartment and collect his whisky. On the way back he noticed the jiffy bag on the side containing Kelly's possessions and on an impulse decided to find out Kelly's explanation of the items significance.

Once alone Kelly used his free hand to unfasten his artificial hand. The exploding box of chocolates in Catherine's flat had not only destroyed Sheryl's phone but also most of his right hand. He always wore the gloves to conceal his injury. He left the Velcro loose and used the remains of his hand to stop it from slipping off. This was the first time he'd felt grateful to have lost a hand as well as an eye. Perhaps he'd get to exact his revenge after all. What was it they preached at the reform school—an eye for an eye?

Lathom banged on the bathroom door and Kelly took his razor from his boot and slipped it up his left sleeve before loosely pulling on the artificial hand. He repeated his monkey walk to Lathom who re-cuffed his hand and told him to sit on the chair.

Kelly let the cut-throat razor slide down into his left hand and carefully opened it.

'Hey, this cuffs too tight—can't you slacken it off a bit?'

Kelly wriggled the remains of his right hand inside the artificial one and felt the hand and cuff fall onto the chair behind him. His left hand was now free and held the open razor.

'OK—stop complaining.'

Lathom put down his whisky glass and leaned over Kelly's shoulder with the key in his hand, at that moment Kelly sprang up and slashed Lathom across the face. Lathom staggered back and tried to defend himself but he received a cut to his hand followed by a blow to the head from the stump of Kelly's right hand. He fell to the floor and Kelly kicked him hard in the head. Kelly picked up the key from the floor and removing the handcuff from his left hand, handcuffed Lathom and, as he regained consciousness, propped him on the chair. He laughed out loud but cursed when he saw his sunglasses broken on the floor.

Lathom's head was pounding, his vision blurred, and he was disorientated. He knew he was in serious trouble. Kelly sat opposite him on the bed where he'd been sitting only a few minutes before, sorting through the items from the jiffy bag.

'Glad you've woken up. I was getting bored with no one to play with.'

Kelly's smile made Lathom cringe. He could feel blood from the razor-cut running down his cheek.

'What shall we play?' asked Kelly and cut off a lock of Lathom's hair with the razor.

'How about chess?' asked Lathom. 'That's a good game. You'll have to unlock these.' He rattled the handcuffs.

'Not my sort of fun.' Kelly smiled leaned over and placed the razor under Lathom's ear. 'Ever see *Reservoir dogs*? Excellent film — but not nearly violent enough for my tastes.'

Lathom swallowed hard, and replied, 'Sorry, I prefer documentaries.'

'I'm getting to quite like you Mr Davies. It's a pity it'll

be such a short friendship. What's your real name? I'm sure it's not Geoff Davies.'

'Lathom, Robert Lathom.'

'Lathom — no wonder I thought I recognised you on the pier. Didn't they used to call you Bob — or was it Bobby?'

'Both.'

'Well, well, after all these years. Time hasn't been very kind to you has it? You've got fat and didn't you used to have red hair?

Lathom shrugged and at that moment Kelly's phone buzzed with a message from Lewis: Melville and Sheryl were still on the ferry and it was just leaving Seacombe. It would be thirty minutes before they got back to the Pier Head and at least thirty-five minutes before they were back at their apartment.

'I forgot to ask. What happened to Dean?' Kelly closed the razor and sat back on the bed.

'Man in the lift?'

'Yes.'

'Dead.'

'I should really be angry. You've no idea how difficult it is employ scum these days. Everyone wants to work in the city or be on reality TV — but I do appreciate a professional.'

'I aim to please.'

Kelly sighed. 'I'll miss you, Bobby — you don't mind me calling you Bobby do you?'

'Feel free.' Lathom knew he was about to die and felt strangely relieved by the inevitability of it. He'd had many a sleepless night over the years replaying scenarios such as this in his mind, but now it was for real he was resigned to his fate.

'I'd planned to work out my frustration on you,' said Kelly, 'I'm sure you appreciate that would only be an enjoyable experience for one of us.'

Lathom shrugged.

'You realise I can't let you go? You've tried to kill me and caused me a major headache with staffing. So you've got to die—but how?'

Lathom shrugged again. 'Bullet in the head?' he suggested.

Kelly tore off a strip of gaffa tape and stuck it over Lathom's mouth.

'Sorry, Bobby, but I need you to still be alive when the police arrive. Then while they're getting the ambulance and securing the building, I'll have time to get away.'

He checked his watch.

'The Lone Ranger and Tonto should be arriving at Woodside any minute now. That means they'll be back here in about twenty-five minutes.'

He sorted through the items on the bed.

'Did you think this was a family album?'

Lathom nodded.

'It's all me.' He flicked through the pages: 'Civil War, Spanish American War then, Ireland, Madrid, Congo and Vietnam.' He shut the album. 'I've missed out a few but I'm sure you get the general idea.'

Kelly handled the gold watch.

'Strange thing is,' he continued, 'it's only these few things that I treasure. This watch belonged to a man called Pearson, a friend of Melville's. The Colt was mine and the Browning belonged to O'Neil—sorry, Flanagan.'

He picked up Lathom's 'Chow Mein' special. 'Perhaps I'll keep this as well?'

He twirled it in his hand. 'Perhaps not.'

He pressed it against Lathom's stomach and pulled the trigger. There was a small 'thud' then Lathom felt as though someone had plunged a red-hot poker through him and stirred it around. He tried to scream but nothing got past the gaffa tape.

'You understand I have to punish you for all the trouble you've caused me,' said Kelly. 'Nothing personal but I believe stomach wounds are the most painful and invariably fatal. What do you think?'

Lathom was so consumed by pain he couldn't even nod.

'I'll take that as a yes.' Kelly dropped the gun and stood up. 'Sorry, Bobby, got to go. Things to do and people to hurt. Have fun.'

He pushed everything back into the jiffy bag picked up his hat and pulled it down low over his disfigured face, turning away from Lathom as though about to leave, he paused and picked up the razor, which lay on the bed, and put it in his coat pocket.

'I nearly forgot. If you get to see the Dynamic Duo before you die, perhaps you could pass on a couple of messages for me? Tell Tonto that I killed her sister — it didn't take much just a thick pillow. And tell the Lone Ranger that I killed that woman of his back in 1918 — held her down in the bath and slashed her wrists — after I'd had my fun of course.'

He tipped his hat and smiled. 'See you in Hell, Bobby.'

Kelly walked to the lifts. He'd originally intended to go to the ground floor and kill that stupid concierge — he didn't want any witnesses left alive—however, without his sunglasses he'd be very conspicuous on the Strand and the killing would have been easier with an extra pair of hands. He stared at Dean's body, which was blocking the lift door, and changed his plan. He rolled the body over. Dean had a cut on his forehead, which had clotted, and a chest wound. Curious, Kelly reached down and poked a finger into the chest wound then licked his finger. He pulled a face and was about to spit when he heard a groan. So Dean was still alive. He smiled—perhaps his recruitment worries were at an end? To make sure, he spat into the chest wound.

Next, he dragged Dean's body fully into the lift, pressed all the buttons from 12 down to ground then pushed the pot plant in as well. As the door closed he waved at Dean's body and said, 'Au revoir, Tweedle-dean.'

Kelly took the other lift and selected the 2nd floor and left the block by the side entrance. He was already walking through Chavasse Park when the lift and its gruesome cargo arrived at reception, and he was crossing St James Street when he heard the first sirens. Within minutes he was back at Rumford Court where he checked his phone and then his watch. Lewis hadn't texted him from Woodside as he'd told him to. Well, perhaps now that Lathom was out of the way, he'd have time to train his thugs properly. He put his hat on the desk and hung his coat with the gun in its pocket over the chair then he opened the wall-safe and removed his passport, which he tucked into his coat pocket. When Lewis got back they'd take the girl to his industrial unit and he could take his time with her—then he'd go back to the States to lay low for a while and plan his revenge on Melville.

He went into the bedroom where the girl lay on the bed, her hands and feet bound, gagged and with a hood over her head. He'd used some of Chan's drugs to keep her quiet overnight but now she was regaining consciousness. He ran his hands over her body and felt her stiffen then pulled off the hood and stared into her petrified eyes. She looked at his disfigured face and whimpered and he smiled; he loved that look of terror in his victim's eyes.

Kelly heard a car pull up outside and, looking through the bedroom window, saw his 4X4. Lewis had arrived and they needed to leave as soon as possible before the police cordoned off the area. He grabbed the girl by her hair and pulled her upright by her ponytail. Then he put the hood back over her head. The front door slammed.

'Bring the car closer to the door, Lewis,' he called out. 'I'll bring the girl.' Then he whispered to the girl, 'OK Rapunzel — time to go,' threw her over his shoulder and walked into the living room.

Back at the apartment building, Peter had been struggling to get free for some time and finally managed get the gaffer tape off his mouth by rubbing it on the edge of the desk. He called for help. Finally he heard voices outside the door and one of the residents broke the door down and set him free. He was in the middle of calling the police when he heard a scream from one of the residents, as the lift doors opened and Dean's body fell out.

Peter knew that he had to act immediately if he was to save Natasha. He grabbed the machine-gun from beside Dean's body and called the other lift, which arrived almost immediately. He took a deep breath and pressed the button for the 13th floor. He could feel his heart beating in his chest and hear the blood pumping in his head. He stared at the heavy machine-gun in his hands and felt out of his depth, but he couldn't go back now. The lift 'pinged' and the door opened.

It was eerily silent on the 13th floor. Peter tightened his grip on the machine-gun then suddenly realised that he didn't know how to fire it. Did it have a safety catch? Where was the safety catch? Was it on? He examined the gun and recognised it from the video game he had played with Ben. He knew how an Uzi coped with zombies — but what about vampires? The door to 13C was ajar and he crept through the apartment, sweat running down his forehead and his fingers slippery on the cold metal of the gun. The last time he'd done this he'd only been risking his pride — now it was his life. He pushed open the bedroom door with his left hand and there was Lathom slumped in a chair, covered in blood. He dropped the gun and ripped the gaffer tape from Lathom's mouth.

Lathom looked at Peter through half-closed eyes.

'Hide my gun,' he murmured and nodded at the 'Chow Mein' special at his feet. Peter pulled him off the chair and unlocked the handcuffs and Lathom leaned against the bed clutching his stomach and panting.

'It was a robbery that went wrong — understand?' Lathom gasped.

Peter brought a towel from the bathroom and tried to stem the blood.

'Take it easy; the ambulance will be here soon,' he said. 'Don't worry about anything else.'

'No!' Lathom snapped. 'Don't you understand? If you want to see your girl again, don't mention Kelly and hide my gun.'

Peter put the gun in his pocket then went to the intercom and called down to reception to tell them to send the police and an ambulance to 13C.

Sheryl was sitting in the driver's seat of the 4X4 and watching the ferry in the distance as it sailed down the Mersey. She licked the blade of her penknife clean and then tucked it back inside her bra. Then she checked her make-up in the rear-view mirror and straightened her wig.

'Who'd have thought blood could taste of chip fat?' she said out loud, then added, 'OK girl time to get this show on the road.'

She started the 4X4, pushed the selector into 'drive' and followed the road signs for the Mersey Tunnel.

She emerged from the tunnel by the small side exit on the Strand and waited for the traffic lights to change. Then she heard the sirens. The lights changed and as she drove down the Strand towards her apartment block she could see the flashing blue lights. Driving slowly past, she counted three police cars and two ambulances. Whatever had happened, she was too late.

She regretted being so selfish. She should have just killed Kelly's thug straight away and not drunk any of his blood. Perhaps then she'd have been in time. But fresh blood was so difficult to resist and it made her feel energised. Ah well, no good crying over spilled blood, she thought. She pulled off the road and parked next to the 'Baltic Fleet'. How would she find Kelly now?

Sheryl searched through Lewis's belongings on the seat next to her. She'd already gone through his wallet to find change to pay the tunnel toll. He hadn't had a gun with him, which had surprised her but had made things easier for her and her trusty penknife.

The only thing other than his phone and bunch of house keys was a bank card in the name of Lewis O'Reilly and a small 'Yale' key with a '3' on the key ring. Bobby had once said that he'd been to a flat owned by Kelly somewhere near Old Hall Street but the trouble was: she couldn't remember exactly where. She could remember him saying something about a cobbled courtyard and the Confederates but, right now, she didn't have time to drive around randomly. Kelly had won this round — Pete would lose his girl after all. That was unfortunate but that was the way it was. Pete's girl was, ultimately, no different from Lee's 'Emmas' or her own 'hot dates' — just another victim. She started the car and was about to turn around and drive back to pick up Lee from the Pier Head when she noticed a button on the dashboard marked 'SAT-NAV'.

She pressed it and an American voice said, 'Please set destination.'

Sheryl looked through the options, scrolled down to 'HOME' and pressed the button, and a few minutes later she pulled in Rumford Place.

'Destination is on right in twenty yards,' drawled the SAT-NAV.

She turned in through the archway and parked in the cobbled courtyard.

'Arriving at destination 3 Rumford Court.'

'Thanks hun, couldn't have done it without you.' She blew a kiss at the SAT-NAV screen then took the key and walked round the courtyard until she came to Number 3, over on the far side a little way from the car. She wished she had her coat with her now because it was quite cold in the courtyard and the wind gusted around her. She unlocked the door to Number 3 as quietly as possible and gently pushed it open. She stepped into the apartment and was creeping silently down the short corridor towards a half-open door when the wind slammed the door behind her with a loud 'bang' and a voice from inside shouted.

'Bring the car closer to the door, Lewis.—I'll bring the girl.'

Pushing at the half-open door she found herself in a small sitting room furnished with heavy leather furniture and lined with dark wallpaper. It seemed as though she had stepped back in time. A large mahogany desk stood against the wall next to her and on it was a large computer screen. Next to the screen there was a black hat and a jiffy bag. A black coat was hung over the chair in front of it. She recognised the jiffy bag. Poor old Bobby, she thought. Quietly extracting the Colt from the jiffy bag, she unwrapped it from its greased paper and turned the chamber to line up the percussion cap. At least Bobby had one surprise left for Kelly and his thugs.

Kelly came into the room carrying the girl.

'Didn't I tell you t ..' He froze.

'Surprise, surprise! Have you me missed me hun?' She pointed the Colt at him.

'Shouldn't you and the Lone Ranger be enjoying the picturesque views of Birkenhead Docks?' he asked with a smirk.

'I know babe, had to tear meself away. I was worried you might slip off before we had time for a little chat.'

He looked her up and down. 'I don't remember asking for fancy dress. Who are you supposed to be?'

'Marilyn Munroe.'

'Really?'

'Who are you then — Phantom of the Opera?'

Kelly laughed. 'I do like you — but don't bother waving that antique at me. It hasn't been fired for over a century. You can't get bullets for it; it needs a ball, powder an ...'

'A percussion cap?'

'I'm impressed — but you still can't get them.'

'Want to bet?' She pulled back the hammer cocking the gun.

Kelly hesitated. The girl was wriggling on his shoulder.

'Even if it's loaded, you can't kill me — but you know that.'

'Perhaps I don't want to kill you?'

'What then?'

'Just blind you — You once said eternity is a long time to be hiding in the shadows. It's even longer when shadows are all you know.'

'I do like your style. We're so alike you and me. Two peas in a particularly vicious pod.'

'I'm not a psycho like you.'

'Really? Where's Lewis?'

'In the back of the car.'

'Dead?'

Sheryl nodded.

'I really should be angry,' said Kelly. 'You and your friend are causing me considerable recruitment problems. I wonder what else we have in common?'

'Nothing.' She wanted to get this over with.

'Who was the first one you killed? Family was it?'

'Step-father,' she muttered.

'Snap!' shouted Kelly, 'You see, we're so alike. Ditch the Lone Ranger and come away with me; we could have such fun together. He's much too pious for you.'

'What do you mean?'

'How about hypocritically virtuous, or sanctimonious. I think that sums him up pretty well, don't you?'

'I don't understand?'

'Don't you? I'm sure he's always going on and on about how guilty he feels about all those people he's killed. He probably even feels guilty about me—but he keeps on killing, doesn't he? He's a hypocrite, nothing more nor less.'

'We have to kill; it's what we do.' Sheryl felt agitated. Kelly had a way of talking that undermined her.

'The difference with you and me is we enjoy it,' Kelly smiled. 'Don't we?'

'No.'

'Really? What about Lewis? Did you have to kill him?'

'No—I mean yes—I mean, does it matter?'

'Of course it doesn't matter, not to you or me. That's the point. Neither of us feels guilty—unlike the Lone Ranger. I bet you don't shed any tears for your victims, do you?'

'No.'

'They're disposable?'

'Yes.'

'Even this one?' Kelly indicated the girl over his shoulder.

'Yes—no!' Sheryl snapped out of her daydream; she levelled the gun at him.

'You disappoint me.' Kelly sneered, '- still so attached to your family.'

'What do you mean—family?'

'You haven't realised yet—who this girl is?' He laughed unpleasantly.

'She's Pete's girlfriend.'

Kelly lowered the girl onto her feet and took off the hood. Natasha blinked momentarily, blinded by the light and disorientated by the drugs. There was no mistaking the resemblance; Sheryl knew immediately that this girl must be Michelle's daughter. The resemblance to her sister Jeanie was uncanny. Sheryl quickly regained her composure.

'Let her go or I'll blow that eye out,' she said.

'Still pretending it's loaded?'

Sheryl saw Kelly glance at his coat on the chair then back at her and the gun. Suddenly he pushed the girl towards Sheryl and dived for the gun in his coat. She instantly side-stepped the girl and pulled the trigger. The bullet hit the desk just in front of Kelly's outstretched hand and he froze, then he spun around and grabbed the girl around her neck pulling her in front of him.

Sheryl's only hope was that Kelly had no idea that her gun was now empty. He retreated across the room dragging the girl with him and Sheryl kept the gun trained on him. She crossed to the chair and, maintaining eye contact, used her left hand to search the pockets of his coat.

'Well, well,' said Kelly, 'you're full of surprises, aren't you?'

She extracted the Browning from his coat so she now held a gun in each hand.

'Let her go, then you can crawl back into your sewer—but don't ever come back or I'll have that eye of yours on a stick in me cocktail.'

'I really think you would as well,' Kelly laughed then added: 'You couldn't imagine the Lone Ranger saying that could you? You're far more dangerous, Tonto.'

'Why do you call him the Lone Ranger?'

'He's smug and self-satisfied and he gets all the credit. Tonto always rescued the Lone Ranger and did the dirty work but got none.'

'So why am I Tonto?'

'Small, tanned and dangerous.'

'Let her go—now!' She pointed the guns at Kelly's head.

Kelly tightened his grip on the girl, who whimpered. He could easily snap her neck and Sheryl knew it.

'We have here what they used to call a 'Mexican stand-off,' said Kelly. He seemed slightly amused by the situation.

'Let her go—or else!'

'You want the girl; I want my things. Let's make a deal shall we? Let's all go out to the car. You bring my coat, hat and the jiffy bag and I'll bring the girl. Then I'll take my things and leave you with the girl—and you and the Lone Ranger can live happily ever after.'

'You won't come back?'

'I promise—Scout's honour.' Kelly made a half-hearted attempt at a scout salute with his artificial hand—while still maintaining his grip on the girl's throat with his real hand.

'Were you in the *Scouts*?'

'No.' Kelly laughed. Sheryl didn't.

The three of them shuffled out to the car. Sheryl tucked the Colt in the jiffy bag containing the photo album and watch and placed it on the passenger seat on top of Kelly's coat and hat. She kept the Browning trained on him. He gradually released his hold on the girl, slid into the driver's seat and started the car. Sheryl grabbed Natasha and pulled her to one side. Kelly opened his window and pointed the Colt at her.

'You promised!' said Sheryl, 'remember — Scout's honour?'

'But I wasn't in the Scouts.' He cocked the gun.

'I know — and I also know there aren't any bullets in that gun.'

He laughed. 'I do like you, I really do. Give my best to the Lone Ranger.'

He started to drive out of the courtyard then stopped and leaned out of the car window.

'See you around sucker!' he called, beeped the car horn which played 'Dixie' and drove off at speed.

Sheryl used the landline in Kelly's flat to call Melville and, by the time he arrived in his Range-Rover, she'd untied the girl and started to coach her on what to tell the police.

'What happened?' asked Melville.

'Just made a deal with the Devil. I'll explain later — what happened at Castle Dracula?'

'Bob and one of Kelly's thugs were shot but they're still alive — just. I assume Kelly got his things back?'

'He did.'

'How do you know?'

'I gave them to him.'

She locked the flat and got into the passenger seat of the car and Melville started the engine.

'Shouldn't you say, "Hi Ho Silver and away" first?'

'What? You're in a really strange mood tonight. What's got into you?'

'Sorry—just a bad joke. Take me home.'

That evening they shared a bubble bath in a suite in the Hilton Hotel on Chavasse Park opposite their apartment building. The police had sealed of the 13th floor while they investigated the crime scene so it was a temporary move. They'd both given a statement to a harassed young detective constable, after making sure that it tallied with those from Peter and Natasha. Lathom was critically ill in the Royal, and without his evidence the police assumed that it was an attempted robbery gone wrong. Sheryl sipped her cocktail while Melville sat with his whiskey glass propped on the edge of the bath. He was deep in thought. She lifted a foot from under the water and flicked bubbles at his face, breaking his concentration.

'Stop that!' he tried to sound angry but a smile gave him away.

'Can I ask you something, Lee?'

'What?'

'Do you feel guilty about all your 'Emmas'?'

'Why do you ask?'

'Just curious. Do you?'

'Yes, I suppose I do—sometimes. We all do, don't we?'

'Yes—yes, of course we do. But not Kelly.'

'He's a psychopath; that's the difference. We're not.'

'No—of course not.'

He stood up to get out of the bath. 'I'll go and get dressed then we can get something to eat. Don't be too long.'

'OK Kemosabe. You saddle up Silver and I'll put on me war paint.'

He stared at her and shook his head.

'What's got into you today? Are you feeling ill?'

Twenty minutes later, Melville was sitting on a sofa looking through Lathom's photo album when she emerged from the bedroom looking immaculate. The jiffy bag and the Webley were on the seat next to him.

'There's some old photos of Liverpool in the Seventies, and some of Bob and his friends.'

Sheryl sat on the arm of the sofa and looked over his shoulder, stroking his hair.

'God, look at that one!' She pointed at a photo. 'I remember when the Liver Building was black, before they cleaned it up.'

He turned over the page.

'Looks like a Christmas party—that's Bob in the middle.'

'He looked quite fit then; I didn't realise he was a 'ginge'.'

She looked more closely at the photo then suddenly recognised the girl that Lathom had his arm around. She took the album from Melville and closed it.

'Come on, Lee—I'm starving.'

It was nearly a week before Lathom was considered well enough for visitors. Sheryl and Melville waited outside the ITU ward and she passed the time by eating the grapes they'd brought for him.

'Lee, now we know Bobby's going to be fine, can we have a holiday?'

'Where do you want to go?'

'Somewhere dead romantic.'

A nurse pressed a buzzer and opened the door. 'Come to see Bob have you? This way.'

They followed her down a short corridor to a private room.

'It seems our Bob has friends in high places,' the nurse confided, 'The police came to see him a few days ago—a stroppy young DI throwing his weight around—but he was only in there two minutes then he comes out to make a phone call and we haven't seen a sign of them since. Then we get told to move him to a private room.'

She pushed the door open, adding under her breath: 'Don't tire him out; he's still very weak.'

Lathom was propped up in bed surrounded by a spaghetti of tubes and wires.

'Hiya, Bobby, brought you some grape ...' Sheryl looked at the sorry remains of the bunch of grapes and hid them behind her back then sat down on a chair next to the bed.

'Believe the police have been to see you?' Melville sat on the other side of the bed.

'Sent him off with a flea in his ear. Cocky sod.' Lathom whispered hoarsely. He laughed then started coughing.

'What is it, Bobby?' Sheryl laughed, 'Do you know where they buried the body?'

'There was more than one.' Lathom replied—then began coughing again.

'Soon have you up and about Bobby.' Sheryl hid the remaining grapes under her chair.

'What happened to Kelly and the girl?' Lathom asked.

'She's fine—but Kelly got away.'

'Pity. I'd have liked him to have paid for what he did.'

'Don't worry, Bobby; you'll soon be good as new.'

'No I won't—they found something else when they operated. They cut it out, but it'll only come back. Kelly may not have killed me but the Grim Reaper's still waiting in the wings, sharpening his scythe.'

Sheryl started to witter on about second opinions and miracle cures but Lathom cut her short.

'It's not me he needs to pay for; we're even. I tried to kill him and failed and he did the same.'

'Then who?' Melville asked.

'Kelly told me to pass on a message to each of you. Lee—he said he killed a woman of yours in 1918. Held her down in the bath and cut her wrists. Is that true?'

Melville said nothing. Lathom turned to Sheryl.

'He said he killed your sister, Sheryl. Didn't take much, he said, just a thick pillow.'

'Bastard!' she spat with hatred in her eyes, then she muttered something about a 'cocktail'.

'Sorry,' said Lathom, 'but you deserved to know it all.'

'There's something you need to know as well, Bobby. You knew my sister too—in Liverpool in the Seventies. Her name was Jean Malone. I saw her photo in your album.'

Lathom muttered something under his breath.

'There's something else, Bobby. She had a daughter—your daughter, Michelle.'

'Michelle?' He started coughing again.

'Yes and *she* had a daughter and her name is—Natasha. She's Pete's girl, the one with the red hair.'

'You sure about this?' asked Melville and gripped Sheryl by the arm.

'Yes.' She shook away his hand. 'We need you to get better and help us, Bobby. Help us get even with the bastard.'

'I can't, Sheryl; there's no way—I'm going to die.'

'You don't have to die.'

'What do you mean?' Lathom's mind was racing.

'NO!!' shouted Melville.

'Why not?' Sheryl turned on him with anger in her voice.

'He doesn't understand.'

'About what?' Sheryl snapped, 'about all the guilt? God give me strength — Kelly was right about you.'

'What about me?'

'Nothing.'

'What?'

'Leave it. This isn't about us — it's about Bobby.'

She turned to Lathom.

'You understand, don't you, Bobby?'

Lathom nodded.

'It's up to you Bobby — yes or no?'

She took the penknife from her pocket and opened the blade.

RECIPES

SCOUSE

Scouse is not only the nick-name of the inhabitants of Liverpool and their dialect but also their 'national' dish. It is believed that the name is derived from *lapskaus* which is a similar dish brought to the city by Scandinavian sailors in the 19th century. It shares many similarities with Irish stew but has its own distinct flavour.

Every family in Liverpool has their own recipe, all are different, all equally good. This is Michelle's.

THE MALONE FAMILY RECIPE.

1kg Lamb casserole meat.
(Beef can be used — but not by the Malone's.)
1 tablespoon of oil.
2 large onions.
2 large carrots.
4 large potatoes.
2 beef stock cubes.
Worcestershire sauce.
Pepper.
Boiling water.

Remove all visible fat from the meat and cut it into cubes. Peel and cut the onions and carrots into small chunks. Peel and chop the potatoes into medium chunks.

Heat the oil in a frying pan and brown the meat in small batches, transferring it to a large casserole dish once sealed.

Add the chopped vegetables to the casserole dish without browning.

Add a litre of stock made up with the boiling water to the casserole dish. If necessary add a little more water until all the ingredients are just covered.

Add a few splashes of Worcestershire sauce and some pepper to taste. Don't add any salt at this stage because the stock cubes can be very salty. Adjust the seasoning prior to serving.

Stir gently and bring to the boil, then reduce the heat, cover and simmer for about four hours or until the meat and vegetables are tender. Check periodically that it isn't drying out, and add boiling water sparingly if necessary. Traditionally Scouse is thick stew and the potatoes should be allowed to break down to provide body to the dish.

Serve with crusty white bread and butter, and either picked red cabbage or picked beetroot.

LIVER BIRD COCKTAIL

3 measures of 'Liverpool' gin.
1 measure of vermouth.

Stir the ingredients in a mixing glass with ice. Strain
into a martini glass and garnish.

Garnish variations:
Sheryl's: up to 3 maraschino cherries.
Lee's: a single green olive.
Kelly's: a lychee impaled on a cocktail stick.

Illustrations

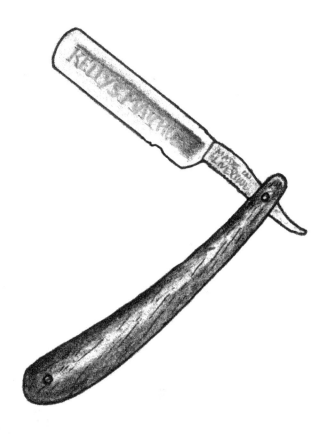

Above: 'Kelly's Matchless' razor

Opposite: Map of Ferry Cruise

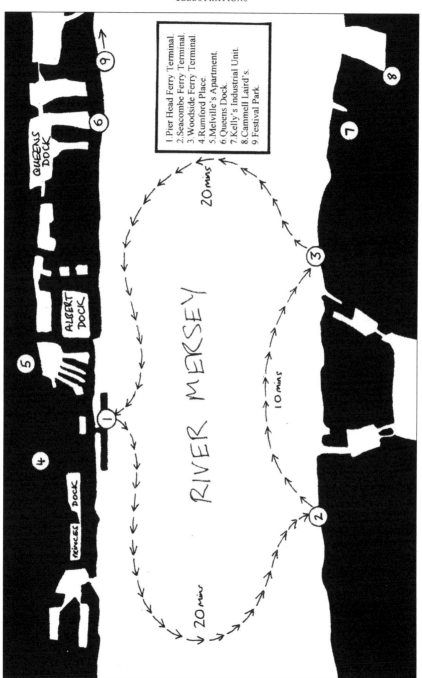

1. Pier Head Ferry Terminal.
2. Seacombe Ferry Terminal.
3. Woodside Ferry Terminal.
4. Rumford Place.
5. Melville's Apartment.
6. Queens Dock.
7. Kelly's Industrial Unit.
8. Cammell Laird's.
9. Festival Park.

'George the Dragon'

'Paddy's Wigwam'